Love, in the Baptism of the Storm

I0594438

Bill Brown and Nosyarg

Heart Space Publications
PO Box 1085
Daylesford, Victoria, 3460, Australia
Tel +61 450260348

www.heartspacebooks.com
pat@heartspacebooks.com

All rights reserved under international copyright conventions. No part of this book may be reproduced, stored in a retrieval system, or transmitted in any form or by any means electronic, mechanical, photocopying, recorded or otherwise without written permission from Heartspace Publications.

Whilst every care has been taken to check the accuracy of the information in this book, the publisher cannot be held responsible for any errors, omissions or originality.

© Bill Brown and Nosyarg 2020

ISBN 978-0-6486524-4-1

Published in Australia

CONTENTS

PREFACE

The world bustles, neighborhoods bustle – flashing lights everywhere, countless young men and women rushing every which-way. Music, songs, loud noise, and traffic pervade the night. It seems a paradise but it's anything but that.

The material life in cities has long consumed the fragile flesh, and values have diminished. Material life that has been thrust upon them must be embraced, where the soul is no longer their own. The authentic people are in rural areas, around the rivers and lakes, the fields, and the land.

The city people have lost compassion, respect, and love for the people who share the streets with them. Perhaps love cannot add anything to the material world, but they do say, "Love makes the world go around" – how lucky for us all. At least if we have the capacity to love ourselves, then perhaps we can love another? However, as this story unfolds, you will see that love can be hard to find, and that the searching for it leads our protagonist to catastrophe.

She, like the other people in the story is young, and young people invariably make mistakes. This does not mean that young people are deliberately reckless but they must take the time think about it, or disaster may occur. If you have no regrets, life is much easier.

Although love cannot solve all problems, we need love, just as much as we need oxygen to breathe, water to drink, and food to eat, for without love, life has no worth. Subconsciously, our protagonist knew this, but her hungering for it left her battered. It seems obvious to most that romantic love is within us, bursting to be expressed, like flowers awaiting spring. It has been like this for thousands of years and ensures procreation. And so, even though our heroine is pushed this way and that, she knows that even with all the failures, finding that one perfect love is far better than never having experienced love at all, than never having tried to find love.

Notes by the Australian Publisher

This story is set in China. To retain the Chinese favour of the story, colloquiums and slang have been retained, but with an explanation adjacent to these in brackets.

The story is situated in China's Dongguan region and gives readers a fascinating glimpse of that country's culture in this day and age. Yet love, its pain, and the never ever search for it, and its finding, is the same in all countries.

CHAPTER 1
BRIDGE SIDE ENCOUNTER

One morning in late autumn, Enzo drove his child to school. It was gloomy, a cold wind buffeted the car, and rain squeaked the windshield like footsteps upon sand. He drove with caution to ensure the safety of his child, only around forty kilometers an hour. The weather affected his mood, and he slowly breathed a sigh of relief when his daughter was safely dropped off.

 Heading towards his place of work, the sky began to lighten up, but the cold wind still howled. The trees on the roadside rustled, waving a frantic dance to an unseen conductor. Because of the excellent insulation of the car, the wind could not be heard, so the experience was an eerie one.

Driving across the frost covered bridge he quickly scanned the water below to assess its mood. Some days it invites you to jump in and swim. Other days, it looks like a fairy tale with fog and limited light, where he expected to see unicorns on the riverbank. Today its mood is foreboding. The wind chopped the surface – grey and white caps ripple with short bursts across the surface. Returning his focus to the road ahead, he vaguely sees a form sitting on the edge of the bridge, legs dangling over the edge. At first he thought the figure was a cleaner or maintenance person. As the car got closer, he saw that it was a young woman. She was hunched, and clearly distraught, unaware of the cars that passed her by as they seemed to be unaware of her. As he traveled this bridge numerous times every day, he knew every shadow, and opening. He could see that she was sodden-wet and wind-blown but seemed oblivious to this. He knew something was wrong – very wrong. '*What is the girl doing there*'? At the thought his heart trembled.

He slowed down and parked at the end of the bridge where the road widened, and ran towards the woman. In the distance he could see her flimsy top and hair blowing. He had an ominous premonition and ran faster, until he got closer. Then gently, like one would approach a stray puppy, slowly approached her. Shouting above the wind, he did his best to have a supportive tone, "Girl, what are you doing here? In such cold weather, you must be freezing? Why don't you go home to dry clothes and warmth"? Although she looked at him, she did not seem to register his presents. He could see her face, blue from cold and blotchy from many tears.' She was nervous, and her body shivered. He tried again, "Come, sister… I'll drive you home".

This time there was a response, and with a trembling voice she shouted, "You…you…don't come any nearer or I'll jump… Do you hear?" She edged closer to side of the bridge.

This scene is no stranger to Enzo, sadly he had seen it all too often in his work as a high school teacher in a sub-economic area. It seemed to be the result of the difficult lives of our time. Teenagers and young adults are the most vulnerable.

Research that he had read indicates that the number of suicides or attempted suicides from this age group was on the rise, and steeply so for the so-called, *Millennials*. The pace of life and the uncompassionate society can be too much for them. They feel frustrated and not heard, especially when their parents and society take no heed of their issues, but how can they as they have their own issues to attend to? To a young adult or teenager, suicide seems to be a statement of despair where they want to be heard, because everything revolves around them, and so in an act of defiance and strength, they think, *'Well, watch what I'll do, you'll be sorry'*. But that is not the answer. They think not so much about being dead in the long-term, but more about making a statement, and, he knew that girls tend to try to kill themselves more often than boys.

Enzo stood still, and slowly squatted down to her height, thereby reducing her fear of him. "Girl, I know what you are feeling… believe me, I have been in the same condition myself. Please… please listen to me… another few minutes will not make any difference to you. I can see that you hurt on the inside. I feel your sadness… know your frustration…… anger… I also know that right now you cannot see one reason to live… You have come to the conclusion that you want the pain to end, and this is how you are going to do it. You think, all you have to do is to slide over the edge of the bridge, and in a minute or so it will all be gone from the cold and water. You think the quiet and gentleness of everlasting sleep will solve your problems".

Staring at him, with bulging eyes screeched, "What would you know… you can't feel what I feel. You've not had the shit I've had. What the hell do you know? What is left – when hope is destroyed... nothing, no purpose or reason?" With this, she burst into tears of such remorse she shuddered all over, but she had not jumped, she had listened, and she had responded to him. His voice was reaching her, and she was allowing him to. He continued, "Can I come and sit next you... I'll not touch you, I give you my word".

Still blubbering, whilst staring at him she said nothing. "I'm coming,... trust me... please trust me", he said as he slowly crawled on hands and knees and sat close to her – her eyes never leaving his.

"Thank you... ...I am returning from dropping my daughter, Sangru, off at school... She's fifteen years old... in a few years she will be your age. It always worries me, how can I be a supportive daddy to her when she goes through some of the things that you probably have gone through. I don't know how I can help her. So, please let me help you so I know better. Please, don't end your life, it would sadden me... I would have failed her. I know how much I would die inside if my daughter jumped... I know how much your parents would hurt if you jumped. In many ways their life would also end if you jumped, and..." As he said this, a much stronger gust of wind blew. He quickly reached out and grabbed her as it nearly buffeted her over the edge. At that moment she also grabbed at him. Their eyes locked – hers bottomless with despair. His reflected concern. She saw only compassion and that he would not hurt her.

Without a word, and with a mutual understanding, he helped her scramble back onto the bridge. As she was safely away from the edge, she thrust her arms around him and buried her head in his chest, great sobs shook her body. She clung so hard he had difficulty breathing. He, in turn, cupped the back of her head gently in his hand and allowed her cry. Soon his neck became saturated in her tears and snot. Both were oblivious to the rain and passing traffic.

They did not know how long they held each other – after a time her sobbing subsided, but the whimpering continued. Slowly, she began to let go of him as she tilted her head to look up at him.

He gently patted her back and comforted her, "Cry girl, right now that's the best thing that you can do. But come, the car is warm, let's go and chat there".

His heart was aching for her – about twenty-four years old, she looked like a little child, scared, vulnerable, like a dear that had been caught in the headlights of an oncoming car. She sniffed in a bunch of snot, and nodded okay, as they started to rise. Slowly, Enzo walked her to the car with a supportive arm around her.

Sitting in the car, he turned on the motor to warm and dry them both. She was pretty, with long hair and big eyes. Her face was a little swollen, but showed the pain of her short life – her unusually light skin exacerbated the red blotches from crying. Her eyebrows were well shaped and covered her almond shaped, brown eyes. Wearing her light shirt and jeans she looked like a university student.

He gently asked, "What's your name?"

With a big sniff she said, "I... my name is Murong... What's yours?"

As he handed her a box of tissues. "Everyone calls me Enzo... Do you feel like talking? To tell me why you're so sad... and wanting to end your life?   Perhaps I can help you. I'm a school teacher and have seen what you are going through... Sadly, it's all too common these days".

She wiped her tears and nose with a tissue and stuffed the used tissue in one of her jeans pockets. "No, I don't want to talk about the things that happened, not now anyway... But I have no reason or want to live. I will go now, or sometime soon... it's all the same to me".

Having said this, deep, long yawns erupted from inside her. She was overcome with tiredness. He suspected she was exhausted from the cold and the emotions that anguished her. She needed warmth and a place to rest her head.

'Where are you living?" He enquired gently.

She replied in almost a whisper, "Nowhere... I have nowhere to go," as she stared blankly through the droplets of water running down the car window. Fresh tears surfaced, rolling down her cheeks, with every so often an uncontrollable shudder.

Enzo considered her situation, and asked her, "Do you trust me... I mean, are you willing to come to my house and stay until you are feeling better... to get warm? My family would be happy to help you for a while. At least until we find a solution, one that you are happy with".

She looked at his hands, which were lightly resting on the steering wheel. Seeing his wedding ring she nodded silently.

CHAPTER 2
FIRST LOVE

For two days he let her settle. Mostly slept and kept to her room, only emerging for meals and the bathroom. Sangru, Enzo's daughter was delighted, as it was like having a big sister in the house. Being a fun fifteen year old, she soon had Murong laughing and coming out of her depression. He waited for her to come to him, which she did after dinner on the third night.

He settled her with a steamy cup of tea, and one for himself. His wife, Feiru, and Sangu, excused themselves and went off to bed to give them privacy. Slowly, as she relaxed, she began to reveal her past. Her story was told in a lineal way. It was emotional, and filled with shadow and pain.

Murong was thirteen in the 1990s, when her parents left Dongying in the Shandong Province to go to Dongguan to find work. She was to go to school there. From elementary school to junior high, she spent in Dongguan. Because of where they were from, they were seen and treated as foreigners. At that time, the local people of Dongguan were wealthier than her folks, yet, they were of a lower class of people, without education, and saw fit to bully outsiders.

Because her parents worked long hours, they had no time to take care of her, and when she did see them they were always moaning about her. She would respond with anger and insults. Soon it became intolerable.

As a foreigner, she studied in a private school because the public schools only accepted local people. This private school was a last resort and badly run. The teachers were without motivation and did not care about the students – all they wanted was their salary, and to go home at the end of each day. There were a lot of dropout's that the government schools had kicked out, who ended up in this school. These were the kids who were angry with society, pissed off with their parents, and their rules. They were rude and disruptive in class, and gave the teachers a hard time. They slouched, were rough, insolent, and aggressive. All who went there hated the school and the non-interest of the teachers. None of them wanted to be there, but were forced by law until they were old enough to leave at fifteen. Many of these kids were on a direct course to becoming tomorrow's criminals and thugs, and Murong became one of them…

"Well, I had to", she said, "I had no friends, and if a young girl has no friends she will find them in any society. My parents didn't support me and allowed me to run wild. I was just as angry and sullen as the rest and found it *cool* to be rebellious".

She was soon swearing, something that she never did before. She smoked and drank alcohol. Often, she found herself, either protecting herself or annoyed with someone, so she brawled often. She and her friends spent most of their time in a bubble net, (an Internet café) playing games, and watching porn. With a big sigh she said, "We wanted to integrate into the gangs or triads. This was really stupid as they were totally out of control fighting each other to become the dominant gang. Because we wanted to make an impression, our group of girls were called *The Flying Girls*… (a euphemism for; loose girls) I was a Flying Girl! 'I was proud of that".

She spoke about a time when in junior school when she met a boy named Wang Weihong. He was a local thug, and had notoriety amongst all of the kids. At that time, many called him Hong Ge, (big boy, the boss). She was in a bubble net café when he walked in. She and her friends were teamed up to play Counter-strike (a popular Chinese computer game). One of the guys next to her told her that he was Hong Ge. At first, she didn't care much. Later though, when they finished the game, Hong Ge loudly announced, "I am paying for everything tonight at the KTV karaoke, the drinks – the lot". Because he was paying, the word got out and many would go. She went with the rest of the crowd to the KTV building (in a KTV, there are many rooms, and groups rent a separate room, just for themselves and their crowd). They had their own room. Always, in a KTV we smoked and got drunk… Things were always better when we were drunk. Booze seemed to make us stronger… braver. We thought we stood taller… what a joke! That night's drinking was different as we were mixing with *the big guys*, and especially Hong Ge!

Hong Ge was mucking around with some of his tough looking buddies. Murong's group stood a little distance away and she got the chance to observe him. He was about 170cm tall, lean with wide shoulders, dark skin, a brown-red hedgehog hairstyle, a sparkling silver necklace around his neck, and a few tats of dragons on his hand. He looked like the underworld boss in a gangster movie that he aspired to be. She realized that her rebellious nature had nothing on this guy… he was the real-deal. She found him fascinating, about twenty-two years old – he was cool, and she was attracted to his rugged good looks. As he joked with his thug-mates, he was confident, and clearly the leader of the gang.

"We flying girls wore sexy, close-fitting skirts, pop-up bras to make our small breasts prominent, our nail were painted black… we wanted to be provocative". We smoked and drank booze, and giggled a lot, and swore with every second word. We wanted to be noticed by the thugs, "It was heady stuff for us fourteen year old's." And Hong Ge made all of their heads spin with his underworld charm and power.

Everyone was singing and dancing, faster and louder with each glug of alcohol. When they got tired of dancing, they stopped to drink more, and eat the snacks that Hong Ge ordered. After a while, Hong Ge, holding his beer bottle by the neck, thought he would try his luck and sauntered across and sat at Murong's table. After taking a slug of beer, he took out a cigarette and placed it in his mouth. As he lit it, he tilted his head slightly and squinted through the smoke, never taking his eyes off her. He inhaled long and hard then blew a line of smoke directly into her face and said, "Hey sexy, where's the boyfriend"?

Annoyed because of his attitude, his arrogant blowing of smoke in her face, and his belittling her. I should have told him the 'get lost'. But I was confused. I felt like a child and wanted to be older, and be seen as sophisticated. I was drawn to stay, so I said, "What's that got to do with anything?" I wondered why he asked me that question, and the fact that it came from the man I was becoming obsessed with.

He said nothing but smiled a knowing smile that said, "You have no boyfriend, it's written all over your face. You're a virgin and playing the big time". Standing up, he told me to wait, while he headed off to the bar. He ordered more drinks, but he took a long time as he was chatting to mates. At one stage they all laughed and looked my way. One of them slid something into his hand, he turned his back on me, towards the bar for a few seconds.

He finally returned and handed me a glass of wine.

"I didn't order this," I protested.

"Just drink it... I got it for you because you're such a beauty," He said enticingly. As I sipped the wine, he began sweet-talking me. I knew he was and again, I was annoyed, but eager for it at the same time, falling deeper into his spell. I began to feel light headed – the room was spinning, my mind went blank and I felt sleepy.

I vaguely remember being half dragged, half carried out of the room, and into another – and flung onto a bed. As my clothes were roughly removed, I could hear myself moaning,

"No please don't," but I was powerless to do anything. The nightmare continued. Although determined to resist, the dream that I was in continued, unabated. I tried to open my eyes and get up. I was too drugged to move.

The memory of the rape brought tears to her eyes. Enzo suggested she take a break and could carry on with her story tomorrow, but she wanted to get it all out, to purge herself of the trauma of her past, determined to continue as she wiped her eyes and blew her nose.

I felt a weight climb on top me. He was laughing as he began to press himself into me, "Feel what I have for you young beauty", as he forced his way, I felt a burst of pain. I tried to scream, but my brain and tongue were divorced from each other. In and out he jabbed, faster and faster, more and more pain… it went on, until with a loud groan, his heavy weight collapsed on to me.

I blacked out. Later, when I began to emerge from the fog, it took me a while to realize who or where I was. I had a pounding headache. It was hard to move. I fell asleep again. When I woke up, I could see it was light outside. Hong Ge was on the other side of the bed, snoring. I had no clothes on, they were scattered on the floor, as if by a cyclone. He was also nude, his back very hairy.

Rolling over to get off the bed I saw a bloodied spot on the bed. I knew it was my blood. My entire vagina throbbed as if a truck had been through it. Touching it with my hand I felt a mixture of semen and blood. My head still throbbed and I collapsed back onto the bed and burst into tears. I was frightened and felt like I was three years old again and in trouble... a big tough *flying girl*, what a joke!

As I sobbed, I must have woken him. After a time he turned around to look at me, smiling that ugly, wry smile of his. He looked my body up and down, and touched a breast. I recoiled and pulled the blanket over me. He laughed and stood up to get his cigarettes. As he stood next to me he lit one, and said, "Open your eyes, I got something to show you... Go on Beauty". In anger I did, and saw that he was front on, his penis just a few centimeters from my face. It was massive, and, as if it had a mind of its own, started to thicken and rise towards the ceiling. He took a deep breath of smoke, and then slowly blew it out, smiled and asked, "How are you feeling? Want to go again?"

I grabbed the bedside lamp in anger, and tried to kill it. He, stepped back just in time as the lamp whizzed past. Again he laughed, and again he took a drag of his smoke. I shouted, "Look at my blood, look at what you did... one day I'll get you back, I swear!"

He laughed again, even louder, "Your threats are funny... so you gonna call the cops? Is that it? Or do you have a scary big brother who's gonna come at me in a dark alley?" He began to laugh so uncontrollably, he had to support himself against the wall. A scowl replaced the laughter, as he composed himself, "You dare call the police," He spat, "What do you think will happen to you if you do? Besides, look at you... look at your clothes... look at your gang name... *The Flying Girls!* Do you really think they'll listen to a slut like you? We – you and I, are the same... we're nothing in their eyes. So what if you lost your flower... and drew a bit of blood...it was going to happen to you anyway. Get over it or we Dongguan people, will get over you"!

He ground out his cigarette as he climbed back on to the bed with a smirk on his face. He straddled over me again, fully erect as he determinedly grabbed my arms and pinned them up above me. I knew it was useless to resist. I simply didn't have any fight left in me. My body was no longer my own. It was his to do with as he pleased.

Once on me, he softly kissed my lips, as he eased himself into me. I shuddered with pain, as he moved, more tenderly, in and out. He stroked my face with his hand, whispered, "Gentle... I'll be gentle... relax, don't fight it".

A week later he sent me a text. For that week I had existed in a daze, doing everything on auto pilot. Although I went to school, I have no idea of what we were taught. At one stage I burst into to tears and ran out of the classroom. I was no longer the body of ice and jade. Until his text came, I thought he was just playing with me for a one-night stand.

There were many texts, saying how much he wanted me. I had mixed feelings... I was hurt and angry but also confused. I started to convince myself that what he had done wasn't so bad. Maybe I would learn to like it now that I was a *'full'* woman. I ignored his texts, but kept thinking about him. A month later, when my period did not come, I was beside myself with worry.

One day, as I was walking home from school, he pulled up next to me in his flashy car. He opened the door and said, "We are going swimming" as he showed me a skimpy, bright red swimsuit. As he said this he looked me straight into the eye, and we both burst out laughing...

We went to Chang'an Stadium, where there is a full sized Olympic pool. He went to the men's, and I to the woman's change room. I was amazed, the swim suit fitted perfectly, but probably cheekier than I would normally buy. Looking at myself in the mirror I felt brave. I turned sideways and was proud of my breasts, each pear sized and firm. I ran out and jumped into the water. He jumped in after me with his knees up to splash me with a bomb.

We were swimming around each other, playing... giggling. Every so often his hand would stroke my breast underwater. My nipples got hard. Suddenly, he pulled me to the bottom of the pool, and then held himself against me as he kissed me. It felt good, so I kissed him back before we rose back to the surface. We stood, pressed against each other and kissed. As I kissed his neck, I could feel his erection. The security guard came to the edge of the pool and blew a whistle and told us to separate.

My parents were angry with me because I had not been going to school, and they could see that Hong Ge was a bad element, and so I started staying with Hong Ge at night.

Whenever he was free, he would pick me up in his car, often, giving me gifts. He was my first love, and he seemed to also love me. I didn't expect it to be so nice. When I asked him what he did today he avoided me, and would change the subject, or would say, "What you don't know, won't hurt you". Loving him was like shooting up heroin. I knew how dangerous it was, but I could not help myself.

When Hong Ge was with me, there was no sign of his gangster activities. I think he was really in love with me. After I became his woman, other small-time gangsters showed me respect, no longer yelling at me like they used to, which embarrassed me at the time. I liked the respect this gave me. The prestige... the queen of his empire. Hong Ge was *the* gangster and nobody was going to fuck with him.

My period had still not arrived. I was worried. I told him I may be pregnant. All he said was, "Get rid of it! You're only fourteen... You can't have a kid. I know someone who will do it".

I needed to be sure I was pregnant so I went the local hospital. It was crowded. I was tested positive and as I left the maternity section the doctor walked out with me and said I must tell my parents However, standing right next to me was one of my mother's work friends. She soon told my parents. Of course, my parents did not want a scandal and they kicked me out of the house. They are of the '*old school*', and worried more about what people would say, than about me, my feelings or health. Chinese people can be so inhumane sometimes. I had no choice but to live with Hong Ge, and so had the abortion.

Murong teared up with the memory and Enzo put a gentle hand on her face and said, "You don't have to tell me about that", as he got up and offered her a fresh cup of tea. They decided to have a break and took a walk in the garden.

CHAPTER 3
WARFARE

After tea they went back into the sitting room and Murong continued her story.

First, Hong Ge was a small time gangster, but was growing in stature – he was becoming noticed in Dongguan. Soon though, he opened a casino and a clubhouse, and then another small casino. As his standing in the gangster community increased, so did mine as Miss Dongguan. Every day though, I had competition with many girls wearing sexy clothes and heavy make-up. Arriving in taxis they would parade themselves around his various establishments, hoping to get noticed. They all knew   the casinos and clubhouses belonged to him. Hong Ge's gang members had all the sex they wanted as these girls vied to be accepted and like me to enjoy the notoriety.

One day, one of his henchmen rushed in and told us that his first casino, on Taishideng Street, had been raided. Apparently, a large gang from another area was muscling in to drive Hong Ge out of business. When Hong Ge heard this, he smacked his hands together in frustration. He got up and staggered off, leaning against the wall for support. His head dropped towards the floor and the ends of his mouth turned down. His breath came in gasps. He then realized that everyone was watching him, and so quickly pulled himself together, "We'll see about this", he said and shouted to some of his men to follow him to the casino. I did not ask, but also ran and jumped into his car. He was so angry, he seemed not to notice me.

Once entering the casino, we saw some of his men badly beaten. Several of the hostesses had been rounded up and raped. There was also a lot of damage to the premises with broken mirrors and bottles. The tables and chairs had been chopped with a meat cleaver – this I learnt was a specialty of the Guangdong area, from which this gang came.

Upon questioning his staff, he was given a message. He was told that a large gang from Guangdong was moving in to the area, and if there were any reprisals, he would be put out of business.

After what I saw and heard I couldn't help but be a scared. I was standing behind Hong Ge and holding tightly to his clothes. The ladies were all sitting on the sofa, crying... their hair in a mess. The stools and table all had chop marks.

Later, Hong Ge learned that the name of the triad boss was Long Ye. Hong Ge knew of Long Ye, as he heads one of the largest gangs in China, and is especially well known as the 'Head Snake' (underground boss) of Dongguan. There was a time when Long Ye tried to encourage Hong Ge to go in with him and work for him, but Hong Ge had his own aspirations. So this was now the first, of what could become a long and bloody campaign. Long Ye was determined to take over Hong Ge's growing business.

Of course, Hong Ge had a few plans of his own for Long Ye. He had no interest in giving up what had taken him years to build. Now that it was booming, Long Ye thought he could just walk in and take over, but Hong Ge would fight to the end, if necessary. Hong Ge had been expecting this attack, but perhaps not so soon. He had also begun recruiting guys, who, for a price, enjoy war – like any good commander he had been preparing for fierce battles. Hong Ge, knew that like Sun Tzo had stated in 'The Art of War', you must pick the battle ground, and so he was going to take the fight to Long Ye's own home, and attack him on several fronts there.

At this time, I began to have strong and ominous premonitions. I was scared. I had heard the stories of the vicious nature of Long Ye and his men, and knew that to weaken his foe mentally, he began with a campaign of torture to eliminate those close to their commander. Because of my role as *queen*, I was a marked girl. This savage and scheming man could have me abducted, but I was also scared for Hong Ge. He was young and impulsive, and although clever, he could miscalculate, and that would be the end of him. The consequences were unimaginable... I started to become an emotional wreck and often reminded Hong Ge to be careful of Logn Ye's tricks. Hong Ge didn't listen. He just laughed it off by saying, "Do you think I am afraid of this man? Don't be afraid for me! I will destroy him!"

Even though he made these brave statements and plans, the pressure was telling as his behavior towards me changed. He became critical of everything I did, and he hardly made love to me. I could not predict the consequences of this war, nor the outcome, but I did pray silently in my heart. I hoped God would bless Hong Ge to defeat Long Ye and his gangsters.

One night, with his men well-armed with machetes and iron bars, it was clear they were going on a raid. I told him that Long Ye's men would be waiting, and happy for the reprisal, as they were picking the battle ground, and would be ready. Hong Ge scoffed at this. I said I wanted to go with him, to support him if something happened to him. He refused to let me go saying, "What can a little girl like you do?" … and then he locked me in a room with no windows. As he did, he told me to be optimistic for him and the outcome, "Fighting is man's business… read your love stories until I return, victorious. Stay here and wait for my good news. My Sunspot (second in command) will be here, watching you, and to look after you". Then he was gone.

In the room there was not a sound, the silence was another enemy. I could not focus on anything with a million bloody and gruesome images kaldeidscoping my mind. My heart pounded as if I was going to have a heart attack. I was so frustrated and angry. I punched and kicked the door that kept me locked in. I gave up eventually and lay on the floor, in the fetal position, whimpering like a puppy without food. My eyelids prickled, my gut swarmed with worry, and my throat was constricted from crying.

At that time, I was not sure if I was really frantic about Hong Ge's life, or my own. We had been together for eighteen months. I was worried about what it would be like without him... not being the Queen. I liked being the Queen! I felt an ominous premonition, as my eyelids started jumping. From past experience, I learned to listen to the fluttering as things would soon go sour.

An hour later, there was no news. Sunspot came in every so often to check on me and each time he came in, he shook his head to indicate no news. The longer I waited the worse the outcome was presented in my mind. Every minute, and then every second was stretched-out-torment. Like a huge stone in my heart, weighing it down... Beads of sweat, as big as rain drops, kept falling from my forehead. My back was soaked, and t-shirt wet. I felt like I would suffocate.

I knew the real reason why he locked me in; it was not that he did not want me to be with him, it was to protect me. But he said nothing about this.

All I could think of was how to escape, as I simply could not sit around whilst my lover was being chopped up. Perhaps he was already dead. What if they were torturing him... how many fingers would be chopped off already? But how to escape? I couldn't bear to wait while he met his death. If I could escape, at least we could die together. No matter what the outcome, I had to go.

I called Sunspot and said that I needed to go to the toilet. Reluctantly, he let me out and led me into the cubicle, before closing me in to give me privacy. I tried to escape through the air conditioning but couldn't succeed as it was just too small. There was an urgent knock, and Sunspot yelled, "What's going on in there?" I shouted back that I was okay and just angry. Quickly I searched the cabinet – nothing on the first shelf, but on the second was Anti-Wolf spray (pepper spray). As I walked out, I gave him a blast in his face, aiming at his eyes. He clutched his face in pain, and fell sideways against the wall. I ran out the door.

Outside, I realized that I had no money for a taxi. I quickly took off my shoes, and ran all the way to Long Ye's local headquarters. We had driven past it to scout it out, so I knew where it was. I assumed that this was where the attack was to be. Although winter, I did not notice the icy pavement. After about three-quarters of an hour, I knew it was in the next block, so I slowed down and replaced my shoes.

As I got closer to Long Ye's, I saw several police cars parked with blue and orange lights flashing, a dozen policemen patrolling the area. They had bunting and barriers around the front of the building to keep passing pedestrians and nosy people from the immediate area. Some had bullhorns and told the crowd to disperse. More policemen emerged from the building, leading handcuffed men out. Although they had their heads covered, I could identify Hong Ge's men by their clothes. The others must have been Long Ye's men. I stood by the barrier and watched as they were led into a large police van, and then, they led another who was wearing black jeans and a silver necklace. It was Hong Ge. I thanked God that at least, he was alive. I called his name and tried to cross the barrier but was stopped by a policeman. I saw an ambulance, and the paramedics carrying a blood ravaged person with a sheet over his face.

Suddenly, someone grabbed my arm and I was pulled away from the scene. When I turned, I saw that it was one of Hong Ge's close body guards, so I went with him. As we got around the corner, he told me he had not participated, but followed the fight via a Bluetooth headset. He told me that Hong Ge ran into Long Ye's ambush. As Hong Ge and his men ran in, screaming and shouting, one of Long Ye's men had a gun. The gun went off hitting one of the charging men, but Hong Ge was not hit. It was too late to pull back so he kept charging at the man with the gun, his machete raised, and struck before another bullet was fired. The man immediately fell to the ground, with a massive wound to the shoulder.

I rushed back to the barrier to see Hong Ge being pushed into a police car, which then took off at speed, sounding the siren.

I felt like I was going to collapse. My heart, like jelly, seemed to skip beats. I leaned against the body guard who was still with me. My legs had given way with the grief of a lost relationship. I fainted. When I came around I was lying on that cold concrete, with a circle of people around me. At first I was confused, but seeing the body guard brought back the scene... I wished I did not wake up from this nightmare. The body guard pulled me up and took me to a friend's house, where I would be safe for a few weeks.

Months later, Hong Ge was sentenced to fifteen years in a high-security prison. I supported him, at first, by visiting him in the holding-cells. Seeing him in his prison uniform diminished him. The former hedgehog haircut had been shaved to a number one crew cut. With the guard standing to the side, we talked on phones through the glass. His eyes were dull and dark, as they stared back at me. In a low voice he said, "Murong... I am sorry for you. I've taken you from one life and given you another... one that is not a good life... I should have left you as you were. But I couldn't... you were special, I needed you. I am sorry to disappoint you... You must leave this place, and find another life. You are strong, and clever. You can do this... forget about me... I have no future, and you will have no future if you hang on to me. Go back to school and study, start again... Be normal".

My voice trembled in reply, "Don't say that, I'll wait for you to come out. You made a mistake, and now you will be punished for it. We are still young... I will wait..."

"No," he interrupted me, "this will be the last time I will see you... I will not allow you to visit me again. I was bad for you, I know that. I will release you... to force you away, so you can find another life. Besides, I will also be better off without you... You see, I must get used to prison life. I must follow the rules, and make this my life. If I think of a life outside, and of you, each second will seem like an eternity. I can't do that for fifteen years. For me to remain sane, I must forget you. It won't be so bad in here. It's controlled, and much calmer than the life I had... not going out and fighting as we did... worried about being killed. There is food to eat, a place to sleep..."

I put my fingers to the glass, and through my tears mouthed, "No, as long as you behave yourself, you will come out in twelve years".

He frowned. "Don't wait for me. I am going back to my cell now", and with that he stood up and called the guard to take him back. As the guard led him away, he gave no backward glance. I watched his back disappear through a curtain of tears...

Without him, life was hard. I had virtually no money. His assets were frozen by the court, and his casinos closed down. I lived from day to day, not caring for myself. My heart and life were broken.

Two months later, I received a letter from him, sent from prison;

Murong, I lied. I never loved you. You were just one of many women... you think you were the only one when we were together? With the life I had, women threw themselves at me... and I was happy enough to catch them, use them, and get rid of them when I was tired of them. Don't cry over me.

Do you know what I love? I love virgins, and you were a virgin. I had to have you, and I took you like I would take a piece of cake off a plate...

There was more in the letter, but I let it fall to the floor. Yes, he did have other women, and probably hurt many virgins as he hurt me, but in my heart, not my brain, I know he loved me. The letter though, bought me to my senses and I knew I had to turn my back on him as he turned his back on me as they led him out of the visitor's room. I loved him, there was no doubt about that. I remember reading in a romance once that sometimes people fall in love with the wrong person. It is part of our make up to search out those things that can, and will hurt us. Hong Ge, was one such person.

CHAPTER 4
FRIENDSHIP LASTS FOREVER

Enzo interrupted Murong to get more tea and a snack. As soon as he returned she adjusted her position on the lounge, curling her legs up under her and continued telling her story.

Although I was determined to forget Hong Ge, I was reeling in a dark cloud of my own making. I had no money. The school had long kicked me out, saying that they do not want gangster-girls walking their corridors. I was not welcome at home. One minute, I was the gangster's queen, next I'm about to be thrown on to the street, and I was still only fifteen. Not being a school girl anymore, I knew I must get a job. I am not the only girl to leave school early, and who was no longer a virgin. Sooner or later, I would find someone who was kind and good who would love me for who I am... and not reject me for what I had done. That is what I thought, but it seems that Life wanted to punish me. Life was hard, and remained hard. Although I knew I could not keep my baby, I mourned the loss. How could I have the right to deny her or him a life? This was not an ant to be stepped on. It was a human child... my child.

❖

My first job was in a hardware factory in Usha. I was just a worker on the assembly line. Every day, except for eating and sleeping a few hours I stood at that conveyor belt, where a million, no ten trillion hardware items moved past my eyes. The punching sound of the machinery was endless, and the sound of the grinding conveyer was harsh on the ears. The work was exhausting, and boring. At the end of each day my back hurt. I had a headache from leaning over the conveyer belt and holding my arms out in an unnatural way for fourteen hours a day. I stayed in the factory dormitory, where I would scramble up to the top bunk to grab a few hours of sleep before starting at 4.00 am the next day.

As time went by, I met a few friendly girls in the factory, where we tried to lessen the boredom with stories and gossip. After a few weeks, four of us moved out of the dormitory and into a share-house. It wasn't much, two bedrooms and one living room. The rent was high but there was no choice for the thousands of migrant workers that worked at the factory, all trying to get accommodation.

"Enzo, let me tell you about the girls," As Murong started to talk about them she seemed more animated. First there was Chen Jinrong. She was a diligent and simple Zhanjiang girl who liked to wear colorful hairpins, like an eight year old… but being a farm girl, she was good in the house, cooking, and cleaning – a bit of a mother to the rest of us. Next was GAO Qun. She came from the northeast. She was big, really big, tall and chubby but always with a smile on her big moon face. She was strong and would always speak up against the foreman who tried to bully us. Chen Yuqing was a petite

Maoming girl who spoke quietly and was quiet… so petite she looked like a young school girl, but she was the smartest of us all. She spent her spare time reading, and was so easy to get on with.

So we were four girls, all from different places in China, and with distinct personalities. We worked together, laughed together, and sometimes argued together. We were sisters, and took care of each other in what was a difficult and uncaring world.

I don't know what they thought of me. I told them a little of my past, but they seemed to not care anyway, and welcomed me into their lives and bosoms. Although the work was drudgery, I was starting to feel happier, and the past was more of a cloud of confusion and less painful. I was glad to be with these three girls.

CHAPTER 5
YUQING AND THE PUNKS

As my parents had cut me off and did not want me around, my housemates were my saviors. Without them, I do not know how I would have gotten on. We were all alone, and supported each other. Whenever one had difficulties, we all helped. We had good food and fun together. Of course, four girls all sharing, have their own moods, and worsened at *that* time of the month, but we would just let that one go through it and keep out of her way, until her cheerful self reemerged.

There was no time for men, and to be honest, none of us seemed to want any. I certainly didn't. We were cohesive and needed no others.

One night, when we finished our shift, around midnight, we headed home to eat and sleep. Gratefully, our rental house was only 500 meters away and in a few minutes we would be home. Just as we were about to leave, Chen Yuqing said, "Go without me, I forgot my phone and need to go back and get it". So the three of us wandered home and as we got there, Gao Qun asked, "What shall we eat?"

Chen Jinrong, with a smile on her face said, "Look at what I have", as she showed us a mysterious cardboard box. She opened it slowly, with an excited grin on her face, "Everyone must taste our Zhanjiang specialty. A fellow villager, Ai Wei, from my home town arrived today and brought it for me… for us. Give me five minutes as I heat it… it must be hot".

As Chen Jinrong was about to dish up, with much giggling and joking she looked at her mobile phone and said with concern, "Strange? Wonder why Yuqing has not returned? She should have only been a few minutes behind us".

"So what are we eating?" asked Gao Qun.

With a big grin Jinrong said, "It's traditional Zhanjiang food that we have at our festivals. Have a look… on the outside are banana leaves that grow in the area. This is what it is cooked in, but it is mixed with wormwood juice, and glutinous rice flour, which gives it the green color".

"What's on the inside?" asked Gao Qun.

"Aaahaaa… it's a mix of mashed peanut, sugar, sesame seeds, and shredded coconut… so it's nice and sweet".

"Sounds Yummy", squealed Murong.

"It is, wait until you taste it".

Jinrong again, cast a worried look at her phone, "Still nothing on my phone. I think, let's eat while it's warm, and I will save some for Yuqing, I'm sure she will be in any second now".

Although we were happily eating and chatting, we kept checking our phones and the front door. I said, "It's already half past twelve… where can she be…? If she went somewhere she would have given us a call".

We all felt anxious, and I felt an ominous premonition. My eyelids were jumping as they did when I had these. Jinrong called the number but there was no answer. Then I tried… still no answer. After a few minutes of trying to call, I suggested we should go looking for her.

Chen Jinrong asked thoughtfully, "Should we not call the police?"

Gao Qun said, "I am not sure, but perhaps they would say, it's only been forty-five minutes and they'll laugh at us. Let's go and find her".

Just as we were about to open the door, it burst open with a bang and Chen Yuqing lurched in. Her hair and clothes a mess, she was hysterical. The poor ragged girl collapsed into Jinrong's arms. I quickly closed the door, and we took her into the lounge sat her down. We were all anxiously asking her what happened… but all we heard was sobbing. I went and made us all a cup of tea, and gave Chen Yuqing hers first. We had to be patient, knowing that we would find out soon enough.

After a few sips of her tea she started to compose herself, enough to shout in anguish, "I… I was raped", and with that she folded herself over, head to knee, issuing groans of remorse, "When I came out into the alley", she continued, "I was attacked by three punks. I think they knew I would be on my own. Maybe they heard us chatting before you left. They

covered my mouth, and dragged me around the corner...
you know, where those bushes are... then pushed me to the
ground, two holding me down, while the other ripped off
my pants...." She was now whimpering and staring blankly at
the wall. Her face swollen, and red with tears.

I gave her a damp cloth to wipe her face with but she just
sat there twisting it around and around her hand, staring
at the floor. We were stunned and didn't know what to say,
at first... after all, what could we say to make it better?...
but the silence only lasted a short while before our anger
erupted.

Big-booming Gao Qun shouted, "We need to call the police
now!"

Yuqing heard this, but was in a daze, and said nothing as
she kept twisting the cloth, her hands shaking with effort.
I gently patted her back and said in a soft voice, "Calling
the police may help... but you need to understand that this
place here, Dongguan is a cesspool. Rape happens all the
time. The cops have more important things to do than worry
about just another rape. Calling them would be hurtful...
and I doubt it'll make any difference. Even if they caught
the punks, it will not lessen the impact on Yuqing". I then
spoke directly to Chen Yuqing, and gently said, "Would you
like us to call the police? We will if you want us to".

Still whimpering, she shook her head, "No...no don't".

"We respect your decision" Gao Qun replied, "It will not
make better what happened to you and the police will do

nothing. We will do what we need to now". Jinrong nodded in agreement.

We knew she was a virgin and for this to happen was the most humiliating, and painful event of her young life.

Yuqing, choked up, managed to speak, "They didn't wear a suit (condom)... I... tried to resist, "But they were too strong..."

The room was suddenly engulfed in deadly silence. The air solidified. We didn't really know how to comfort her. After a few more moments of stony silence, I knew I needed to say something helpful, "As your sisters we will stand by you. You will get over this. Girls, please run Yuqing a bath and help clean her up," as I went to my bedroom where I had some contraceptives and disinfectant that I had used before. I took these into the bathroom, and we gently washed the rape away as best we could. After the bath, tea was made, and with the tea I gave her the contraceptive and a pill to help her sleep. We put her to bed, and sat by her side until she fell asleep.

We would take care of our own. We would heal her with love, compassion, and tasty food. We would laugh with her, and cry with her. I knew this pain. I had gone through it myself. You get over it but you never fully recover.

A month later Yuqing's mental state was much better. Our efforts had not been in vain, so our hearts were happier, especially when her period arrived. In order to prevent this kind of tragedy from happening again, I suggested that we were always prepared and must carry Wolf Water, just in case. As Wolf Water is expensive I suggested we make our own. It's easy enough, I checked up on the Internet.

I went and bought a whole bag of chilies, and cheap plastic spray bottles, that were small enough to fit in our pockets. I soaked the chilies for a few days. After straining out the chilies, and adding pepper, we were left with our own brand of Wolf Water. It looked a bit funny but would do the trick. We even practiced with normal tap water where we played punks and good girls, learning to quickly spray the water into each other's faces.

When we were ready, we added in our wolf water, and held it in our hands every time we finished our shift and walked home. None of us ever walked home alone again. Lucky for us, or lucky for them, we were never attacked. Still, we had to be prepared. Life is not easy, especially for the poor, but we lived our life and gained experience as we went along.

CHAPTER 6
SEPARATION OF THE SISTERS

In the blink of an eye, the four of us had spent two years and three months together in that small rental house. We always knew that there would be a day when we would go our separate ways, but we would remain friends forever.

The year was 2008, and we will always remember it as being one of the coldest years on record. Usually Guangdong's winters were mild, but this year, for the first time in over a hundred years, it snowed. It was also the year of the Global Financial Crisis. Because of this, many foreign-funded enterprises in Dongguan closed down, whilst many more were on the verge of bankruptcy. What seemed to be happening was that although many of the factories closed down, the bosses still held the power and still grew rich. It was the workers who suffered, with even longer hours and less pay. Our factory was Taiwanese funded, and we were worried they would pull the funding, so that is why we worked harder for less money... to try and keep our jobs. We lived in fear, and when the managers called a staff meeting, they said because of the turmoil on Wall Street, international companies were not buying our hardware products anymore, and warned us of the factory's imminent closing. No one was surprised. For me, I was not too worried, as I longed for a change, and to breathe fresh air.

Sure enough, our factory completely closed down a month later. The workers in the factory began to go their separate ways. It was all very sad. Also, it was not easy to get a job at that time. The trucks and forklifts in the factory began to transport the equipment out to be sold off. It was demoralizing, watching this once thriving factory, with several thousand people, now empty.

The day we were told not to return the next morning, we sisters gathered in the rental house to discuss future plans. Gao Qun said that her aunt had opened a restaurant and asked her to go and help. Jinrong had graduated from high school, and now that she had saved a little money, she wanted to study typing and get a certificate. She said she would also try and find part-time work in a department store until qualified. Yuqing was the most timid, and more so after the rape and said nothing, so I asked her, "What about you young one?"

She lowered her head and thought for a while, "Murong, I'll follow you".

I smiled and said, "Well, I don't know what I want to do. Are you sure you want to follow me?"

She was a little anxious, but soon said, "Yes... I have no parents since childhood, and only one sister. She often bullied me. Over these last years you have been a *'big sister'*, and taken care of me... so I'm going to follow you. Wherever you go, I go".

I was both pleased and apprehensive, but said, "We will make out okay".

The night before we were to leave each other, as a farewell we went to a KTV in the city. We sang and danced as if the world was soon to end. After consuming four or five beers each, we moved on to wine. The more we drank, the louder and more raucous we got, and we hugged each other with tears in our eyes.

We played until 3.00 am. Gao Qun and Jinrong had to hold each other up – they were so drunk and dizzy. Yuqing was vomiting violently in the toilet. After I settled the bill we stumbled outside. We wanted to get a taxi but the drivers took off when they saw how drunk we were. With no choice, we started walking. We sang all the way, like a group of mad things. Although we were very drunk, the last few months with the extra work to try and keep the factory going had been hard, and with Yuqing's traumatic experience we needed to go out and have fun. To play for one night, our last night together was a good thing. Two hours later we arrived for our last sleep in the house.

We woke, thick-headed, about mid-morning, and packed our bags. After checking out, we were standing and on the pavement as is the Chinese way, we exchanged gifts for each other. We said our last goodbyes. Yuqing and I caught a taxi to the city. I was just eighteen years of age, and it seemed like I had already lived a full life.

CHAPTER 7
CHEN YUQING AND I

I was happy that Yuqing wanted to remain with me. She would be good company, and we could share costs, cooking and cleaning. It would be easier for us both. I never imagined what a good sister she had become to me.

I had a friend whose family opened a foot bath spar. I took Yuqing and thought we would support them, but when there they offered us both jobs as hostesses, we were not sure what that entailed, but soon found out. In places like Dongguan, sex dominates everything, so there was pornography, and girls who offered *happy-endings*. Without this in the back rooms, the foot spar would not have survived. Thankfully, we were not there to be '*a lady*'. As hostesses, we welcomed guests as they came in, gave them tea, and took them to the designated room according to their wants. The work was not demanding. All it entailed was to stand around, talk, smile a lot, and be pretty young things. No matter how tired we got, we still had to appear lively and happy.

They gave us sexy cheongsams to wear (snug, full length, and colorful dress), that fitted perfectly. As we were not *the ladies,* we had to fend off the groping hands of the drunks, and ignore their words of lust. There were guards to look after us, but they were happy to watch the drunks try their luck. As long as they did not get rough with us, the guards did not interfere.

It was not an ideal job, but was better than the factory. Besides, we knew that these places would go on if we were there or not. In some ways the two years with Hong Ge prepared me as I have seen countless episodes, far worse than this. Some days it was fun, chatting and laughing.

At first it was harder for Yuqing, as this was new for her, but it helped her to overcome her shyness. I thought she looked sexy in her cheongsam! So we were at home together, went to work together, and went and had meals together. All the time we seemed to get closer and closer, and before we knew it, we had been working there for half a year.

One cold winter night, with sleet outside, and the wind whistling we watched a movie together. As it was cold, we snuggled under the blankets in my bed. After the movie ended, she yawned, stretched and said, "I'm just far too comfortable... I think I'll sleep where I am". I didn't think much about this and quickly fell asleep.

In my sleep I had a dream, or thought at first it was a dream. Yuqing was softly kissing me. In the dream it felt nice and I let the dream continue. Next, soft fingers enter my vagina and gently massage. This was when I woke up and pulled away. I could not believe what was happening. Yuqing suddenly sat up and quickly apologized to me.

Confused, but feeling nicely wet down there, I asked what happened? She said shyly, "I... want to love you... I do love you, and I have held off for so long that I couldn't help myself. I ... I don't like men, those drunks in our foot shop, and since those who raped me, I can't ever be with a man. I hate men".

After listening to her words, I thought that she was not really gay, but that it was a reaction to what happened to her. I held her hand, but kept my distance, so our bodies were separated. "What you were doing felt nice, but I need to think about it. First let me tell you about my past".

Twenty minutes later I had told her everything. At one stage I had tears in my eyes when I mentioned the killing of my baby, and with real concern she gently wiped my eyes with a tissue. No one had done anything like that since I was little girl. The tenderness that she showed me softened my heart, and I realized that she did love me.

When I had finished talking, she snuggled closer, and in a happy voice said, "You have also been raped, and had a difficult time. Let me look after you with my love... let my heart heal your heart, as you heal mine. For now, let us not think of men". Her hand took mine and placed it in her pajama top, where I softly caressed one of her breasts. Her nipple instantly responded, hard and urgent. She continued speaking, "This is not homosexuality, it is love, and love is normal". Leaning in, her lips brushed mine. First she gave my top lip a gentle bite, and then her tongue crept into my mouth. Her kiss of angel tears excited every cell in my body – I fell deeply into her embrace and lost myself in her love.

❖

I did not remember ever being so happy. Spending my time with Yuqing was like an infinite feeling of belonging. We were inseparable. Like other lovers, we walked the streets holding hands. We did not care about the looks that we got from the many disgusted people. Yuqing told me that same-sex relationships had been legal in China since 1997, but many did not approve and so we faced social challenges. She had never been with another girl before, but knew that *I was the one*. There was one old lady who, in a fit of aggression, tried to unlock our hands and separate us. To tease her, Yuqing ran after her and pretended to kiss her. The old lady ran off in fright. We shrugged the incident off and carried on walking. We also had bemused looks from young men, who probably thought that these two pretty girls would be better served as their play things. We just scoffed at them. We were happy, and we showed it by holding hands wherever we went. We fooled around in shopping malls, cafes and in the cinema, where we watched *chick flicks*, eating sweets together. Men, with woman can kiss and show their love, and so did we.

CHAPTER 8
THE SISTERS ARE IN LOVE

Although we were very different in our characters, we complemented each other, like two pieces of a jigsaw puzzle, different shapes that fit well. She was intelligent and creative. I was practical and thorough. It was interesting to meet our friends... most were supportive, some were shocked, amazed at how happy we were. Some thought it was just the sex – it was so much more than that. It was the gentleness of a woman loving another woman. In some gay relationships, there is a butch partner, who plays the role of the man, the boss, the patriarch. We had no such thing. We were both feminine, both delicate, and enjoyed prettiness. Neither in charge of the other.

A woman's body is softer, with nicer contours, and I adored Yuqing's body. A man's body is gross compared to our satin softness... so tender, with textures only women have. She was younger than me, and so I tended to play a more supportive role, yet, she was wiser than me in many ways.

Murong paused to ask Enzo a question, "Do you have an issue with gay people?"

"If I was a woman, I would be a Lesbian, as I also love woman... my woman, my wife."

They both laughed, and then in a more serious tone, "I have no issues with gay people. I have never had a gay experience... never had a desire for one, but I recognize that others do. It is entirely their choice. I was glad when the government allowed same sex marriages... and after the terrible time you had before, I can understand why you desired the gentleness of a woman".

"Yes, it was good for me and made me feel safe."

After work we would rush home, have a quick meal and climb into bed together. This was a beautiful time of love, nurturing, and talking, watching movies or reading to each other. We talked for hours, or listened for hours as the other had something to discuss or explain. We had the television on a lot of the time and watched our favorite serials, where together we *oooed* and *aahed* at the goings on. Inside our unit it was another world, our world, a safe world, where everything on the outside had no existence, like a lost tribe that had no knowledge of any external beings elsewhere. It was here, at that time, where we healed. Over time, men became less brutish in our minds, and we accepted that there are good and bad men, and that with luck, we would find good men who would give us babies, and love to be a family with us. For now, we had each other and that was sufficient. Tomorrow would look after itself.

There were times when we had days off from work. We would get wrapped up under a quilt and binge on horror movies – often screaming out loud from fright or hilarity. The downstairs residents were constantly yelling at us to "shut up", but we didn't care – we ignored them.

Some of the stories were so real, it was like the ghosts were in our bedroom. Yuqing would get terrified and sometimes held on to me as if the monsters would jump out of the TV to take her – she clung to me as her savior. So real were these, with the graphic images and the music we were *creeped out* but excited at the same time. After one such horror movie, we were so scared that we couldn't sleep. I had to turn on some comedy, even so, Yuqing could not settle so I gave her a sleeping pill and settled her down by holding her. I delighted in the job as the oldest to keep her safe... to keep her happy.

CHAPTER 9
ANOTHER TURN IN FATE

Looking back on the days when I lived with Yuqing, our two and a half years together, were so happy, they flew past. Of course, there were quarrels, but we worked through them in a mature way, and none rankled for long. At the time I hoped that we would always be together and never separate. However, it seems that Life did not like our own arrangement. Since we cannot change our destiny, we had to accept the outcome.

The conversation about having children came up again. We both wanted children. Yuqing was sensitive to my feelings about having my child aborted, and she would console me by saying, "That thug Hong Ge, for once was right, as at only fourteen, and without money or family support, you and child were heading for disaster".

Thank goodness we had no fertility issues, and felt safe in that respect. We both were tested for STD's to see that we were clean after our respective rapes – we were.

Anyway, about children, we decided to wait a few more years, get some money together, perhaps start a little business, and then try and adopt. It is not so easy to adopt in China.

Because of the one child policy, most children are kept by their parents, but there are children, and if one is prepared to spend money, then it can be done. And in this time, we were preparing our minds and hearts for the child that was to come. We started accumulating books on child rearing, and would spend hours cuddled up in bed browsing these books together. We three were going to be a *forever family*. We were about to have our names put on the list of the 'You Too Can Adopt a Child' organization.

Our love for each other was much more real than Hong Ge's version of love. I loved both, but I now realized that they were different. Hong Ge's need was for his own emotional support, and was not aware that I could also have that need. But for me, at the time, I needed his strength and also the false position of his role as a gangster. His position somehow filled me with what I thought I needed – status and being deemed as, *the queen.*

This love for Yuqing was from the heart, based on respect, reciprocal respect. Hong Ge wanted sex and someone pretty to hang on to and make him look good. I needed to hang on to him, to make me look good... how shallow? My relationship with Yuqing was one where I could see deep into her very mind, heart, and soul. There was no ego, just compassion, no competition, only support.

Being the *book-worm* she was, she would read to me, and tell me a million facts that she had learnt over the years. She had to get glasses and being so petite and young looking, she looked like child prodigy. Yet, she had an understated wicked sense of humor, like the time when we had just finished a meal in a restaurant. The man behind the counter shouted at us that we must put our finished dishes on the tray and bring them back to him at the counter. Instantly, Yuqing stood up, and packed the tray, then when she started to walk the eight meters to the man, pretending she had a deformity, whilst the tray and plates rattled precariously. Within a few steps the lazy man saw that his plates and cups were about to end up in a thousand pieces on the floor. He quickly rushed to relieve her of her burden. As soon as he took the tray she straightened up, and said, "Thank you my good man", and then with poise, slowly walked over to me, perfectly, held out her hand for me to take, and we walked out together.

I was delighted to think that this was to last for the rest of my life.

One day, I took Yuqing to climb Lotus Hill. We had heard about this great attraction, not far from the city, but it takes endurance to get to the top. Lotus Hill is in the parklands in Dongguang.

The weather was beautiful. A light spring breeze blew, and it reminded us of the preputial spring of our love. The birds and vegetation on the mountain were prolific, as was the scented wild flowers. We were one with each other, and one with nature. It was as if it blossomed just for the two of us, yet no flower was prettier than Yuqing.

We followed the crowd and struggled up the mountain. We were determined to get to the top knowing that there would be less people there. The climb had us huffing and puffing but we were younger than most and so were able to get ahead. Luckily, there was a café halfway up. We purchased bottles of water, and had a rest under a large Maple Tree, whilst admiring the view. Once refreshed we proceeded. As we got higher, the temperature cooled down but we were hot from our exertion.

It took us several hours to get to the top. The view was breathtaking, as we admired the White Mountain across the way. It got its name because of the constant foreboding and swirling mist enshrouding it. Craggy rock pinnacles came in and out of view as the mist swirled, a mysterious wonderland that surely would defy any who tried to climb them. Away from White Mountain it was cloudless and in the far distance, and on an adjacent mountain, we could make out a Buddhist temple. It looked as small as a matchbox from that distance. We stood, in silence, shoulder to shoulder, arms around each other's back. Thinking that we were on our own, she swung around and gave me a gentle kiss. We then heard a clucking sound, and broke apart. We saw an old man and his grandson. He was smiling and did not seem shocked as most Chinese men would have been. He indicated with his arms that we must continue, which we did.

He went off with the boy, and we could not wait to kiss again. A feeling of joy and love overwhelmed us both and so we continued to enjoy the sweetness of our kissing – for me, I was feeling every part of her body heat, listening to her slight breath, our two tongues enraptured by the tingle of this sensual moment.

We stayed at the top of the mountain for more than two hours, until it was time to go home. Although our legs were fatigued from the upward walk, we held hands and let gravity half carry us down. We laughed and giggled with a feeling of freedom as we embraced life. We were in love, and had the exuberance of our young years, accompanied by this spectacular scenery that spread out far beyond us...

When arriving at the bottom, it was already dark. After such a long day we decided not to cook, but to eat at a restaurant. We wanted to find a traditional place, one where there were local workers. These are cheaper and the food better. As we strolled along the street I had that little ominous prickling of my eyes, the one that preannounces drama. 'Rubbish', I thought, 'Things are just too perfect'.

While we walked, Yuqing was busy on her phone, sending a message to someone, so was a little behind me. As I got to a crossroads the traffic light showed that we had five seconds to finish crossing. I called out, "Yuqing, hurry, let's get this!"

I ran across, thinking she was just behind me. As I got to the other side, I heard car breaks squealing – a hooter blaring – a guttural scream – a bang – glass shattering – and saw the horrified gasps of people. I spun around to see Yuqing flying through the air. Her head crashed into a concrete telegraph pole, and landed with a deathly thud some three meters away. As she came to rest, blood splattered the pavement. Her head was soaked in blood. A pool of blood trickled onto the road.

In a daze, I ran to her, my heart thumping... panic stricken. My legs felt like formless rubber as I collapsed on all fours next to her limp body. I licked my finger and placed it under her nostril. She was still breathing, but barely. I began screaming for help, and with shaking hands, tried dialing the emergency number on my mobile. I was crying so uncontrollably, I couldn't press the 120.

Someone reassured me they had already called. I folded myself over Yuqing's mangled body and whispered, "It's okay Yuqing… the ambulance is on its way … you need to fight…I need you… you must live".

Her eyes half opened, and with blood coming out of her mouth, she gurgled softly, "Murong, my sister… my lover… I…I can't hold on". Her breath was fading away, but she managed to give me these last words, "You have been my greatest joy, I… I will always love you…"

My tears overflowed and I heard myself shouting in desperation, "Yuqing, if you love me, don't leave me! I can't go on, alone without you". She tried a final smile, but her body shuddered as her life was released from her. Her breathing stopped. All was still.

"Nooooo, Yuqing, don't…" My heart, my hands and even my very soul felt like it was shaking. I held her lifeless body, willing her to come back to me.

I don't know how long I stayed there but eventually felt myself being gently pulled away by the paramedics. They attempted to resuscitate her but her heart was already stubbornly wooden. They tried several times while I begged them not to stop. Eventually they turned to me and shook their heads – there was nothing more to be done.

In the screeching of a car's breaks, my world was shattered. In that moment of impact, I went from loving life to knowing that it had ended for me. Life was a cruel beast, and God the cruelest beast of all.

I rode in the ambulance, like a zombie, to the hospital where she was proclaimed dead on arrival. Looking at the body… now cold… now silent… I held her stiff and blue-paste-colored hand in mine, gently putting it against my lips for a last kiss. I tried to say goodbye but couldn't. The words caught in my throat. All I could think of was, 'I should have protected you better.'

Yuqing had no parents, gone when she was a child and I did not know how to get hold of her sister. I organized the funeral. There were only a few of us. I personally took her cremated ashes to her homeland and scattered them in the forest that she so often mentioned. She was goodness in life, and I knew her ashes would help to nurture the forest, as she had nurtured me.

Often I visited her tombstone standing alone on a small hillside in the cemetery. My grief was so deeply embedded, that there was not a day that passed where the tears did not well up in my eyes. My chest ached and depression descended on me like winter in a valley. I visited no one… I couldn't, as my voice would crack and the crying would spontaneously erupt. When I was at her memorial site, I never knew what to say. I was afraid that she was lonely wherever she was, so I burned a lot of toy houses, toy cars, toy puppies, incense, and money, whilst lighting joss sticks to create good shui (goodwill) for her. I also burned a photo of us together, hoping she would be thinking of me.

I had done everything I thought I should do, to let her go peacefully. I did my best. I numbly moved on with my life, but there seemed to be no point… no point to being alive.

Murong paused for a moment, looking pensive as her grief overtook her. Enzo asked her encouragingly, "How old were you then Murong? I think you must have been only around twenty? You were so young to have endured so much!" He leaned over and squeezed her hand reassuringly.

CHAPTER 10
ORDINARY LOVE

The time was close to midnight and Murong had been talking for three hours, and although Enzo did not want to interrupt her story, he had to be up early to take Sangru to school. He asked her if it would be okay to continue tomorrow night.

Murong quickly looked at the wall clock, "Sorry, I didn't realize how late it is. Yes, you must go to sleep, but if it's okay, I can't sleep now. I'll make myself another cup of tea. I will try and fall asleep later".

When Enzo returned next day, he was keen for her story to continue because sometimes there is healing in the telling. As soon as the evening meal had been eaten and cleaned up, he shooed Sangru and Feiru off to give them privacy.

Murong continued…

Most nights I cried myself to sleep, but would wake up three hours later and toss and turn until it was time to get up. I had big bags under my eyes and my health was failing.

I left Yuqing's hometown, Shanxi, and returned to our apartment. I still regarded it as our home. Everything about her was still in present tense. For a few weeks I tried to continue with the job at the foot spar but I was too washed out to deal with clients – there was no smile on my face because I had no smile within. The owners were good to me but finally they had to replace me. After that I just sat in the flat where we had so much fun and drifted through the months. I cried less but my soul had abandoned me. Yuqing once told me that when our soul leaves our physical body, we die. It was like most of my soul had gone, and I was mostly dead, but kept breathing and walking. After a few months I was less sad, but there was no excitement in me. I couldn't remember when I had last smiled. Maybe I was too tired. Maybe I had experienced too much. I had lost my desire for everything and continued like a zombie, a walking dead.

I had almost run out of money when I started to look for work. After a long period of running from one interview to another, I finally found a station ticket seller's job. I was busy on the job and blissfully anonymous in a sea of humanity.

As this job consumed hours but paid little, I could not see it as a long term plan for my future so I decided to attend night classes to study accountancy. The studying helped to fill the void of my empty, nights.

My new routine was, up at 6.00 am – get to work at 7.00 am – work flat out all day, and go straight to college to start at 5.00 pm, then finally, I arrived home at 11.00 pm, and on weekends I studied. Although I was tired, it was fulfilling – I was learning a vocational skill for a future with prospects.

Three months passed by and with hard work, I achieved a basic bookkeeping certificate. Next, I studied for the level of trial balance. I enjoyed the studying, and started eating properly. With the routine, life looked brighter.

A teacher at the college, who often said I was doing exceptionally well, gave me an introduction to a manufacturing company who were looking for someone. I got my first job as a bookkeeper. Of course, I had a six months' probation period, and the starting salary was not much, but it was my entry to being a white-collar worker in an office job.

Fortunately, the company was not far from where I lived, and I enjoyed picking up a ride-share cycle and rode to work. Sometimes I rode home, sometimes I walked, or if the weather was bad I would take the bus. Life settled, and I was not as tense. From time to time, I looked at the photos of Yuqing on my phone. She still lived in my heart, and was forever in my mind. Nights were the worst – once the light was turned off.

I enjoyed the work. It was challenging as my focus had to be pin-pointed. They gave me the title of creditor's clerk, where I processed all the invoices that the company had to pay. There were hundreds of these, from all the suppliers. I had to be careful when checking these bills that they had not been paid before, and that we had received the goods. The last woman was fired because she had made mistakes and it cost the company a lot of money. By Friday, after a week of focus, I needed the weekend to take a break and relax.

I joined a hiking club and made friends, so some weekends we would enjoy a hike or climb up a mountain. These were good times, but they also made me sad as I remembered our time of going up Lotus Mountain.

As time went by, and I mastered the job, I relaxed into it. I gradually made friends with my work colleagues, and most of us got along well. Occasionally, we would go for a drink and a meal after work – it was a new beginning. On weekends, and on the Spring Festival Day, many of us met. We enjoyed nearby outings, went swimming, had barbecues in a park. It was nice to get out and about.

After work one day, one of my colleague, Xiaoli, handed me an envelope. It was addressed to me but there was no sender's details or stamp, so it was hand delivered. I asked her who gave it to her. She just laughed at the mystery. I put it in my daypack and headed home.

Later, after I had eaten, I opened it. I saw a dried red rose inside. The letter was folded into a heart shape. 'Strange', I thought, 'This is a love letter'. I was bemused, but felt a bit weird. 'Who on earth sent this?' I wondered.

Unfolding the heart, I read;

Dear Murong

I have admired you since you came to work at our company.

Whenever I see you happy, I am happy. When I see you sad, which you seem to be often, I am sad.

You are the wind, I am the sand, you are the flowers, I am the tree.

I want to shelter you from the wind and rain.

You are a tea, I am water, together we can be good for each other...

In love Liu Jun xoxoxo

I collapsed laughing. Surely this was a joke? I pictured Liu Jun in my mind. He was tall and nice looking, his hair was straight and a bit spiky. He seemed to have a lot of friends and laughed a lot. He was often in the group when we socialized. He worked in the IT department... something to do with software. But this letter... was it really serious? I remember getting one just like it when I was nine years old! It was from a boy up the road. 'Why did he not give me the letter himself,' I thought, 'He is a big boy. Why do it through Xiaoli?' I was not interested and went to bed.

The next afternoon, when I was preparing to go home, Liu Jun suddenly appeared in front of me. At first he said nothing. The poor man was shaking like a leaf blowing in a breeze. I must admit, I reveled in it, and did nothing to ease his discomfort. I stood waiting with my head tilted slightly sideways.

Finally, the clumsy words emerged, "Mur...Murong. Will you have dinner with me?"

I hesitated before I blurted out, "Thank you, but no thank you. That is nice of you but you do not know anything of my past... and ... and I am not ready to see anyone".

With this I turned to go, but as quick as a samurai, he blocked my way, "Please... just give me one night. If after tonight you don't want to see me again, I'll leave you alone... come on... what have you got to lose..."

My mind was telling me to get out of there... to run away, but then another little voice within said, 'He's right, you have nothing to lose... other than yourself'.

He took me to a nearby French restaurant. It was an interesting place. The seats were cradle-like, like sitting in a swing. He ordered some red wine while we looked at the menu, finally settling on 'Le Plat Principle', a fish dish with vegetables, and a cheese platter to end it off.

While we waited for the food, and slowly sipped our wine, I was quiet. I still thought it may be some sort of joke.... that perhaps friends from work were about to jump out and surprise me, or maybe he just wanted to get me into his bed. I still didn't trust men and wondered if I ever would.

The wine seemed to relax him and he asked, "Do you know much about French cuisine?"

I shook my head, "I'll eat first then I'll know something," I laughed.

"This is the only French restaurant in Dongguan. French chefs use only fresh, seasonal ingredients, and they all like to cook in their own style. This makes eating out a fun experience. They like to serve food that is a treat for the eyes and for the taste buds... a delight for all the senses... the aroma... the way it is presented and of course, the taste... dining becomes more than just eating... it's fine dining..."

I was only half listening, I felt frustrated and wanted him to get to the real point and so interrupted, "You asked me to come here, surely not to tell me about French cooking. I know you want to say something. Please just get it out."

He was a bit shocked at my bold-frustration, but also a little excited, so he cleared his throat, "Murong... I like you... Do you like me?"

"You seem okay", I replied with caution, "but I don't want a relationship... I'm scared of being hurt".

The wine seemed to be making him braver, "I would like something different from love. If you like me, I want to sleep with you". Having delivered the reason for his mission he leaned back in his swing chair and waited.

I was a little surprised and did not expect that he would say anything like this so soon. Perhaps he was more experienced at picking up girls than I assumed. My mind quickly reminded me of the many months of loneliness, and how I wanted to be held. I forcibly asked, "I'm not a virgin, does that worry you?"

"Good, neither am I. You are very pretty and I want to sleep with you."

I couldn't believe what was happening… we were talking about sex as if it was like saying, "Would you like a piece of cake?"… but more amazing, I was seriously considering saying, "Yes". I hit my head to see if I was dreaming. How I wanted to be held. I knew that there is no such thing as a good man, and although this one seemed a bit bumbling, his body was appealing.

"Where will we go?"

"There is a good and clean hotel around the corner."

After that, we said nothing about it and ate our meal. When finished we walked to the hotel. I was relaxed because of the wine, but not drunk. He booked a room and I could not help but smile as he argued for a better price. The room was clean, with a yellow theme, white walls yellow curtains and bedspread. There were pictures on the walls. The room was dull but satisfactory. Seeing a bowel of 'fortune' *cards*, I put my fingers in deep and selected one, *Life is what you make of it*. Well here I was about to sleep with someone I had hardly spoken to. 'So there you go', I thought. At least the mattress was clean, firm and comfortable.

There was little foreplay, and after half an hour Liu Jun finished. I am not sure that I was. It was not long before he fell asleep. I couldn't sleep… my mind was with Yuqing, where we sang together, played together, shared our own happiness, shared own pains together... of how inseparable we were... her soul in my body and my soul in hers, where the merging had been so complete that we seemed as one. As I lay there, next to this man, who I did not care about, tears watered my eyes. Each teardrop was a good memory, 'Now who am I... what have I become... what else I can do?' I thought hopelessly. I prayed silently, I hoped that Yuqing was happy and free wherever she was, 'Please forgive me for not being with you', I spoke to her in my mind, 'I can't do anything about it and must remain here alone to flounder in this life, accepting the terrible destiny that Life has in store for me. I quietly let myself out and went home. It had been a long night of tossing and turning. I knew that I had used Liu Jun as much as he had used me.

CHAPTER 11
HAPPY IN LOW-KEY

My elicit love-affair with Liu Jun was carried out in secrecy, because the company had regulations against staff engaging in male-female relations, let alone getting married. That suited me as I could date him, be held in his arms, but did not have to commit, as it was, in theory, 'just a fling'.

In time, I found myself looking forward to these clandestine nights, where we often skipped the meal and headed straight for the hotel. Each time he would argue with the clerk for a better rate.

Over the months he became a better lover, and was always willing for me to show him what I liked. He was more respectful of my body and my feelings than Hong Ge had been. I was developing feelings for him, and started getting a thrill from his body. I think that he was growing fond of me as well because we often went to movies and restaurants. Liu Jun told me about his previous two girlfriends. The first one was Feng Ling, and apparently, she left him because he was not rich. The second one, Pantene, wanted sex with him and other men at the same time. Lacking confidence, he could not handle that so he dumped her. I felt sorry for him as underneath it all, he seemed a good man.

As the weeks became months, it became increasingly difficult to keep our relationship secret, but nobody in the company seemed to notice anything between us. When we did find ourselves working together, such as when he had to update software in my office, there were no words of love, there were no warm glances, just company talk. The new found joy had to be buried in the bottom of my heart, and I felt like a thief.

Outside of work, we enjoyed shopping together – buying clothes, going away for romantic weekends, and sharing good food. I was given more responsibility at work, now looking after two creditor's clerks and was given a salary increase. I had more freedom and more money to spend on myself.

The feeling reminded me of the beautiful times with Yuqing, although this love was different. Yuqing gave me the emotional support that only a woman could give me. That same sex relationship healed a lot of the pain in me. In the beginning, Yuqing was dependent on me for love and mature support, which I relished giving her. As much as I hurt when she died, she taught me to how to love, and that I realized was her greatest gift to me. With Liu Jen, he was fun, and easy going, and I could be an expanded version of myself. Now, with more money I could expand in other areas than I could with Yuqing.

I then compared Liu Jen with Hong Ge... My time with Hong Ge was both good and bad, love and hate, emotion and pain, but in essence, it was always about him, never about me. These two men were different in nature, education and temperament, but Liu Jen was far more respectful towards other people. The sex with him was different, and it felt good to have a dick inside me. I didn't know where the relationship would end up, but during that time it was easy.

The grief of losing Yuqing will always be there, an inerasable scar. You can never love someone as much as I loved her and get over it, but I learnt that you can still grieve and miss someone and be happy. Just because I was still grieving over her didn't mean that I could not love another, as I was starting to do. There will always be a hole within me... no one can replace Yuqing. I thought of my lady lover with great affection, and it made me sad that I would never see her smiling eyes as they searched mine in love. Yet, I was happy.

Now that I was in a more elevated position in the company, I was enjoying the work. It was busy but not so busy to cause undue stress. I was liked and appreciated by management. Still, there was a deep fear. My life had been ripped away from me twice... surely it would not happen again? When this thought came I quickly erased it from my mind, but it did come... and often, and with this was the tingling eyes that foretold of misery to come. Liu Jen and I had been dating for a year at that stage. Maybe this time Life would have pity on me, and that the *twitching eye* was just an allergic reaction to the spring flowers that were starting to show.

CHAPTER 12
JUST A TOY

As a celebration for our first year together, I took a few of my belongings to his apartment and spent most of my spare time there. It was bigger, and more modern than my unit. It was also in a better part of town. Yet, I could not bear the thought of giving up mine and, Yuqing's apartment. Another happy year flew by. I was now twenty-three years old, which is the age when most Chinese girls get married, or are soon to be married.

I felt that time was slipping beyond me. I was happy, but the thought of having children came again into my mind. It did not happen with Yuqing. Perhaps it would with Liu Jen. I was aware that many of my friends had long been married and already had complete families.

As you know, Enzo, we Chinese girls are primed by our parents and society to marry young and have a child, and when a girl gets past a certain age, she no longer has worth in the eyes of men. Although I didn't want my social conditioning to dictate how I lived my life, it still did. I began longing for something more permanent, and dreamed of being a mother. I started feeling embarrassed, when I went out with my friends, that I wasn't married.

At first I said nothing to Liu Jun, as I hoped that no matter what our company said, that he would ask me to marry me him. I kept waiting… but nothing. Then I could not keep my mouth shut and started dropping hints. Either he was just dumb or pretended not to notice by simply ignoring them… he just continued as normal. The Chinese traditions bit deeper and deeper into me. I got more and more anxious to persuade Liu Jun to marry me. Whenever I raised the subject, he would get impatient and change the subject. Resentment began pushing us apart, and things were not as easy as before.

At night when he was asleep, I would pray to Yuqing to come and guide me, with that everlasting wisdom that she had. On occasions, I felt her presence, and thoughts entered my mind, '*You are good enough Murong, if he does not want you, another will*'.

On one occasion he burst out, "Why do you want to get married so early? There are many people older than us not married. Put it aside, and leave it for another year, then we can talk about it".

I shouted in anger and frustration, "I want children!"

I had not told him about my abortion and how that affected me. When it was out I knew for sure I wanted to be a mother. I wanted to be a mother with Yuqing, and now I wanted to be the mother of Liu Jen's children. Instantly, I knew that my whole life had been for this moment of having children.

I saw all the hurt and frustration of my parents to me, and I knew that the love that Yuqing showed me was inside of me, and all the love that I had for Liu Jen was only a small amount of the love I could shower on my child. I would be a wonderfully loving mother. Life was meant to be shared, and all my hardships told me that a loving family is the most important thing in life. I wanted this. It was not what others expected of me, I was above that – I wanted children.

I tried to convey all of this to Liu Jen, but he laughed at the idea, and so was laughing at me. He asked me, calmly at first, but then ended up shouting at me to pack up my things and go back to my own apartment.

The next day at work he ignored me, but sent me a message saying that he had put in an immediate request for a transfer to the branch office on the other side of town. They had been suggesting that to him for several months, and so it appeared that he submitted to their request. That night, I saw him carrying his work possessions out. I had no choice but to let him go. Every couple of days he would send me an SMS, just to keep in touch, he said. Occasionally, on weekends we met for a walk in the park, but our relationship had become strained and awkward.

Back in my own apartment, I felt Yuqing's energy around me, but missed Liu Jen. I was lonely and watched a lot of TV to pass the time. At night I used the sex toy that I had bought off the Internet. It helped me relieve my desire, but a thing is not the same as a person. Things can't hold you and embrace you. As I masturbated with *my toy*, I felt ashamed. *Good girls* in China do not use such devices, and although my clitoris reached a pleasurable climax, my heart remained empty.

In the long hours on my own I kept thinking to myself, 'Come on girl, you've been here before. You can get over this man'. I reminded myself of what Yuqing said in my mind, *'You are good enough Murong, if he does not want you, another will'.*

There was another reason for my deep loneliness; I was virtually cast out from my family at fourteen years of age, then abandoned from the *gang-family* two years later, then made an orphan all over again by Yuqing's death. If I had to be honest with myself, was that perhaps with a wedding ring I would be secure in a family. I knew this was a foolish belief but I had no control over these emotions, and the sense of abandonment I felt.

I kept my distance from him. If he wanted to go for a walk, I did so, and I answered his SMS's, but other than that, I removed myself as I wanted to get over it. It was like having a cut on the leg, and every time I saw him, it was like pulling the scab off... and having to heal all over again, 'What was it that drove him away? Was it me, was it because he feared marriage... responsibility?'

He kept texting me, telling me how busy he was, and that I was not to bother him, but he was sending me mixed signals – he wanted to break up, wanted to be left alone, but still wanted contact when it suited him. I loved him. I wanted his children, but I didn't want to play his games. I stopped replying. This was hard, especially when his messages became more frequent. He also tried to call me a few times but I ignored them. I was distressed but strong. There was even one time he knocked on my door. When I did not answer, he banged louder. The same people who shouted at Yuqing and I when we cried or laughed at the horror movies started shouting again. Finally he went away, but before he did he pushed a roughly scribbled note under the door. It simply said, *I love you, I am sorry*. I screwed it up into a ball and threw it into the bin. I had enough of his games.

I tried to watch TV but I kept thinking of the note. Of course, I grabbed at the glimmer of hope it offered, as we lost-lovers often do. I decided to visit him the next evening. It was month end, I had to work back a few hours, and so thought I would pop over to his apartment afterwards.

When I got there, I could hear music, but even after my third round of knocking there was no answer. I took the apartment key out of my backpack – I had forgotten to give it back to him when we broke up. As I walked in, I heard the music that he often played when I was there. I was shocked to see clothes strewn around the floor, both his and a woman's. Suddenly, I heard Liu Jun's voice, and the voice of a woman coming from the bedroom. Without thinking, I barged into the room... there she was, on top of him, and for a few seconds their lovemaking was so intense they did not notice me. When he finally saw me, he froze. She, realizing someone had come in, turned around. Her eyes locked with mine, mine with a tear, victory in hers. I threw his door key at her, and ran out, and down the stairs.

What a fool I had been to trust him, to trust God, the God who always teased me. My mind was in chaos. On the way home I bought a dozen beers and drank most of them.

A week after this incident, Liu Jun sent me a text message begging me to meet at the same French restaurant we had gone to for our first date. I told him to go to hell, and never contact me again. Again, my woman's intuition had been correct – the ominous warning of the twitching eye, but I did not expect such a sordid betrayal. Maybe there were no good men in the world.

Murong took a breather from her story and sipped on her tea, turning to look Enzo, "Are there any good men left?... You seem to be a good man. You helped a stranger... you love your wife, Feiru and Sangu. Are there more like you?"

"Murong, you have to believe that there are because there are... You have been unlucky... made some bad choices along the way... look at Hong Ge... that was a bad decision. Your life could have been different if you had left before he drugged you with a date rape drug... but at fourteen you were still a baby and should never have had to go through that. Yuqing's death was an accident, a sad and unfortunate accident... and as for Lui Jen, he actually sounds like he had some good in him... after all, you would not have loved him if there was no good there... but he seems immature, and needs to grow up."

Murong went back into telling her life story, "Since Liu Jun, I was back to distrusting and hating men... can you blame me? I know what you said about Hong Ge, and you are right, I should not have been there... but what about the three punks who raped poor little Yuqing? She was so young. They are all for their own selfish desires. I am angry about what Liu Jun did to me, putting that note under my door to say that he loves me, meanwhile he is fucking someone else. I felt helpless. My fate stalks me, like a dark cloud that hovers over a mountain. Maybe, from the day I was born, God had already arranged my miserable fate and now sits back and enjoys his handiwork!

CHAPTER 13
JINRONG

Again, I tried to restart my life. I continued with the bookkeeping job, and was relieved he was working in another depot. It seemed strange to still be working there as all I did was go through the motions as if that dark cloud was like my dark mood. I said hello to my supervisors and my colleagues with a smile on my face, but my happiness was only skin deep.

My recent break up pain was probably more about all the buried sadness for the loss of Yuqing, and also for the tiny life that had lived in me for eight weeks. Two months later there still seemed to be no reason to live... and why live if my life was going to be like it had always been. Even though I tried to be happy at work, the people around me did notice, "Murong are you okay... you have lost so much weight... girl, you've got dark rings under your eyes... are you okay... you are so jumpy... do you suffer from anxiety?" The list of questions went on and on. I wanted to run away.

Weekends were the worst, when there was no work. I just sat in our apartment staring at the walls, living a life like a corpse. One night when walking home, from just walking, I passed a girl selling jewelry at a street stall. Some seconds after, my mind said, 'Hey, I know that girl'. Without being obvious, I stopped and slowly turned around to double check. I did know that girl but my anguished and tired brain couldn't bring forth her name. I saw some black nail polish, which reminded me of *The flying girls*.

I picked up a ring, whilst trying to remember, pretending to consider buying it. Suddenly I heard a voice I recognized, "Murong... sister!"

I looked up and saw her smiling at me, and remembered just in time, and with excitement called, "Chen Jinrong... Chen Jinrong, my housemate... well, well, well... how are you?"

She replied with equal excitement, "Fancy seeing you here... I am good, but how are you... and how is our little sister Chen Yuqing?"

With that, my voice quivered, tears welled, for a moment I was speechless, "She... is dead... car accident three years ago."

Her joy at seeing me turned to despair. She was quick to say, "Give me a minute..." then she called, "Yena... Yena, come here". A young girl appeared and Jinrong said to her, "Earn some money, look after my stand, while I go and eat with my old friend."

She came from behind the stand and stood next to me, where we embraced, both crying. After a minute she said, "Come, there is a quiet restaurant up the road", and with that we started heading towards it. We said nothing until she asked, "Murong, how many years has it been?" I just shook my head, too sad to try and work it out.

We arrived at the restaurant, and found a table. She ordered tea, and said, "Maybe we eat a bit later. First, let's talk", then very gently she said, "Tell me what happened".

In fits and starts, interspersed with crying from us both, I told her of our time together. She made no comment on our same sex relationship, which I was thankful for. She finished by saying, "Poor little Yuqing... at least she had you, and for that I am sure she was most happy and grateful". After the tea, we ordered wine. We needed it.

She told me a little about her life since she left. I could see that she was not the same free-spirited farm girl. It was five years since we had seen each other but she had aged twice that much. I could tell from her face, her life has been hard.

She told me that after we all went our separate ways she tried to get a part time job so she could study, but she was in and out of jobs; bosses trying to sleep with her; companies going broke because of the aftermath of the GFC. She worked on the land in Zhanjiang, her home province for some time, but there was not enough money... never enough money. So she did not study, and there were no future prospects. She left there and came back to this town, hoping to find work... none came. She borrowed money... and ... slept with men... to get money to start her little stall.

She took a sip of wine and went on to say, "When at home, I met a male elementary school teacher. He chased after me all the time and hoped that I would marry him. I liked him but was unsure. We slept together, and then

I moved in with him. Soon though, I began to notice his many shortcomings. He gambled, and when he gambled his money away, he gambled away the little I had, so I ran away from him. Now, I'm single, getting older, have no money or hope, but I am still young enough, and have a good business brain, and although life's tough, I'm at peace, that what will be will be… Hey, tomorrow is another day", and with that she swallowed the rest of her wine.

With the wine, and the change of conversation from Yuqing and her, we were both a bit brighter. We even laughed a bit. "Murong, we must eat, or this wine will go to our heads. Can I order for us both as I know this restaurant? I remember that you loved to eat green peppered beef. The green peppered beef here is very good. Can I order you some?"

I was a little embarrassed, "You remember that? Wow…I remember the food that you cooked… so yummy. You farm girls sure are good cooks".

She giggled again, and said, "Every time I come here and eat the green peppered beef, I remember you. You were the most organized, and the most mature of us four, so smart… did you know we all looked up to you?"

I was embarrassed, and just shrugged my shoulders.

This was the best I had felt for months. I ordered another glass of wine. We spoke of the good times that we four shared, all the good food, and how Gao Qun scared and chased that horrible foreman. We laughed, and wondered what happened to her?

The food arrived and it was as good as she said it would be. We had a moment of silence, where we were both considering things, then suddenly she reached over the small table and grabbed my hand, and pleaded, "Murong, now that we have met up again, please do not... you won't disappear again?. This place is so harsh, it keeps me down, and poor. I have my little store, but I only make enough money to just survive. That's why I didn't take you to the fancy Western restaurant next door". We laughed at that. She continued, by letting go of my hand and changing the subject.

"This Cantonese food reminds me of the past. Everything in the past seems to be much better than now."

CHAPTER 14
LIFE BECOMES GOOD, AGAIN

Jinrong and I met on a regular basis. Having a friend who was not part of work was refreshing, and I started to emerge from the dark cloud. One night she asked me if I loved Yuqing.

"I did, very much."

"What's it like having sex with another woman?"

I could see that she had been thinking about this for some time but it took a bit of time, and courage to ask me. I asked her why she wanted to know. "Because, even though it seems unnatural, it must be much safer both physically and emotionally…" She replied coyly.

I shared my thoughts with Jinrong and told her about my time with Yuqing, and how gentle and loving it was. This was new territory for her and she listened with interest.

"And did you miss men… I mean their sausage?"

I laughed before saying, "Yes, sure, that is the best part of a man, but on the end of a sausage is the man, and they're not trustworthy, only thinking of themselves". We both laughed, then went quiet thinking our separate thoughts, so I did not offer her anymore, but I did think to myself that it would be nice to have some same-sex love again.

On another occasion we had been chatting about a movie that we were about to see, when suddenly she asked, "And loving a woman, is that easy?" I could see where this question came from, although she had been hurt several times by men, she never thought of having a relationship with a woman.

"There is only one way to know, that is, try it yourself', I said.

We had a quick meal, and then went into the movie. Halfway through, I felt her hand reach for mine. It was nice holding her hand, but as soon as the lights came on, she quickly pulled her hand back.

Over coffee, she asked, "So… what happens next?"

She was a bit shocked when I said, "Nothing… or everything. I don't want you to get hurt… and I don't want to get hurt… again. We need to take it slowly, really make sure we want to be with each other." I had no intentions of pushing her for sex. That is a man's behavior, but as I sat there I was wet between my legs, and I wanted to lay my body against hers.

However, with the honesty of the farm girl she was, she announced, "Murong, I have already thought of this. In fact I have thought of little else since we met up again. I am going crazy between my legs, and want you. Yes, I want you… badly".

I had to ask, "Is it just sex you want because I will give it to you... happily. Or do you feel something deeper for me?"

"Both... You may laugh at this, but when we shared the house, I always felt closer to you than the others. I thought it was just being sisters, but since we have met up again I'm always thinking of you. I see your smile, and know how nice you are... remember how I remembered the food you liked. I think even then there was an attraction, only I didn't recognise it."

"What do you think about us having a first date? Tomorrow night we'll meet in our restaurant, all dressed up, for a 'special' date. We will celebrate with good wine. Then we will go back to my place and make long and beautiful love".

Those twenty-four hours seemed like an eternity. I wanted to hold her so much. Needless to say, it was beautiful. Jinrong was such a willing learner, and kept asking, is this okay? She was delightful. For her part, she seemed genuinely happy. I know I was.

It was not long before she was regularly staying over at my place. I taught her female to female love, and she patiently taught me to cook. We experimented with both. Then one night, I said, "Come... sit here next to me. Are you still interested in studying something?"

With a smile on her face, she nodded a big yes, as she sat down.

"Okay, I will teach you a little about bookkeeping, as it will help you in your business. But first there is a very important thing to do..."

"What", she asked?

"Kiss the teacher", which she did.

Now, this book is called a ledger…"

Although I couldn't teach it all, she had a better understanding which would help her in her little stall, especially as she wanted to grow it from a street stall to a fully fledged shop. Because she could now analyze her profit per product better, it was easier for her to see which items cost more but gave less gross profit.

CHAPTER 15
ALTERNATIVE ENTREPRENEURSHIP

Things were good between us, but there was one issue...
I worked through the day, and her busiest time was at
night and the weekends. It was difficult finding quality time
together.

One night, after midnight, by the time she had closed up her
stall and made secure her stock, I had been waiting for her.
After giving her a meal, and tea, I asked, "Jinrong, do you
think we can really live like this?"

"Um... I love you. Is that not enough? You love me and I
love you, but I still must run my business".

I didn't expect this reply, and for a moment I didn't know
what to say. It seemed that she really loved me. "It makes
me happy to hear that you love me so much, and it makes it
easier to say what I am about to say".

She quickly interrupted, "Should I be worried?"

I just continued, "And I love you, too. But... but I can't bear
for us to be apart, not only for me, but for you as well. For
me, love is not like a meal, where you have a bite here and
there. I have an idea that I would like to discuss with you".

"Oh", she said, fearing the worst, "what it is"?

'You just told me you love me, and now that we have been together for a while you are not so afraid to show that love for me in public. You hold my hand and you shout at anyone who looks at us in a funny way…"

She nodded and wondered where this was going.

"You know that there are many gay people. More than you just see on the street, but they hide and don't show their authentic self… they are scared to. You know that the law allows us to get married. However, the reality is that many, so called *straight* people don't accept gay people. So I think we should open a place to meet the needs of people, like us… I want us to open a gay club. Now, before you say no, look at us, I am strong in financial management, and now have a little bit of money behind me to start it… and you are a natural business girl, you could sell sand to the Arabs, or ice to Eskimo's… and your cooking, that is something else… we are partners in love, and we can become partners in business… and look at how many gay people we can help… What do you think?"

She literally leapt on me with excitement "I love the idea… I love you. You are so smart. Yes, we can do this."

She ran into the kitchen, and came back with a bottle of Champaign we had been keeping, and two glasses, "We must have a toast to our new club". As she poured it, she asked, "What are we going to call our club?"

I hesitated, then with boldness said, "Yuqing's". For a second she looked at me, then with a big grin, raised her glass, "To Yuqing's". We sat up for another two hours eagerly discussing and brain storming our ideas and put together our first draft of our business plan.

The next morning, before I went to work, she said, "I know of a place that I think could be great. I will go and chat to the owner to try get us a good deal. This place was a restaurant but the previous people went broke. They ran it badly, terrible food. It's been standing empty for some time so maybe we can get it at a good price. If so, then you can come along and have a look".

With a quick kiss, I ran out the door, and looked for a bike to ride to work on.

The next day, after work, and with Yena to look after her stall, we went to check out the venue. Good to her word, Jinrong had secured a great deal. Now we just had to decide if we wanted it. We decided almost immediately, we did. It was in a quiet suburb, which was what we wanted, and the perfect size.

That night at home, I filled in a lot more details in the business plan to determine our budget. Upfront we needed 450 000RMB (Chinese currency) to open up and give us six months operating capital. I had about forty percent of the funds that we required so we needed to borrow at

least another 280 000RMB. Once again, my business savvy
partner said she knew someone. So we got another 280
000RMB, and on reasonable terms.

I thought it was a good idea for me to continue working my
current job until we were sure our overheads were being
met. Jinrong, sold her little street stall to Yena, and worked
full time in preparation – decorating, arranging suppliers
and terms. The poor girl was working fifteen hours a day.
I went there every day after work and on weekends. When
I came in, she was always covered in paint, and had bags
under her eyes, but there was always a big smile on her face
when she saw me. She was always positive.

Funnily enough, she reminded me of my father as she was
dressed in overalls, as he always was. Then I thought of my
father and that I had not seen him for far too many years. For
the first time in a long time, I wondered how they were getting
along and promised myself when I wasn't so busy, I would go
back and visit them. I was anxious and craved to see them.

We had great pleasure in designing the sign that was to
announce the name of the club, 'Yuqing's… A club to be
gay at'. This was a play on words because gay, of course,
also means happy. We wanted our gay clients to be happy,
but obscuring the real reason for the club. Under that, it said
'Admission by membership only'. When the sign was erected and
we switched the neon lights on that night, again, we toasted
with a glass of *champers*, both of us happy but with tears in
our eyes. 'If only Yuqing could see this… perhaps she can,'
I thought to myself.

Finally, we were ready to open. The outside of the club appeared to be like any other *normal* restaurant, as we did not want to attract attention from homophobic people. We knew we would have to find excuses to turn people away. For that we hired two of Jinrong's big friends. They were not gay, but were happy for the work. They had never worked for two ladies before, but soon got into the swing of things. We could not believe the challenges we had to face to open a gay club.

I had spent weeks setting up profiles on a few different social media platforms. I did an internet search for gay clubs around the world. I got ideas and inspiration from them, but we created our own look. We decided to use photos of my beautiful, Yuqing, in all her different moods, as part of our style. I could see from these sites that our décor was not going to be as trendy as those international clubs, but we had used our creativity and done our best with limited funds. We were really happy with the result.

It turned out, that the consultant we hired to help us with our décor was also gay. He did not have a partner and could not wait for the club to open. He recommended sea-blue wallpaper with luminous light on the walls. The carpet was a practical light green fleck. We had the chairs and stools covered in a similar tranquil green, and the table cloths, sea blue like the walls. We hung a huge pink heart above the bar, with signage on it that said, 'Make love not war'. It was corny but we liked it. There was a large screen that never was allowed to show politics or sport, only graceful and happy scenes. We put together a DVD slide show of beautiful people, dressed and undressed... nothing pornographic, all natural and sensual that screened on several walls. I was able to bring out my artistic side by painting some of the wall hangings so they matched the décor. I had never painted before and enjoyed the process.

I installed a private membership app on our social media profile. We attracted many gay *netizens*. It was difficult getting them to pay the up-front membership fee for a place they had never been to, but we offered a nice discount for early membership and even a free, once off coupon, for those who recommended one other gay person We sold a few and attracted a new database of potential clients.

It made my heart sing seeing Jinrong in her new role as manager, decorator, cook, and club organizer. It made my heart sing. At night, when we finally collapsed into bed, she covered me with the sweetness of her love. We would often talk into the early hours of the morning. We were happy, but still afraid that we could fail. This was our first business experience, and we were trying something untested... a gay club in China. We didn't dare to be too optimistic. We had already exceeded our budget so we knew that we had to do everything we could to succeed.

Jinrong would just shrug her shoulders, "We can't do more than we have. If it works it works, if it doesn't then... we continue making love and drinking wine".

I kissed her on the forehead before we drifted off to sleep. I loved her attitude but I was still apprehensive... if we failed, there would be no money for wine.

The day we were to open 'Yuqing's', it was a beautiful, clear day. Many of our friends arrived to support us and ordered meals so the cash was already flowing in. Jinrong, was mostly stuck in the kitchen, cooking and giving orders to the new staff. We knew it would get easier, with each passing day. Then, to our surprise, more people arrived … and still more came… beautiful boys and girls. Our free vouchers had paid off, but they paid for drinks, paid for meals, and most of all they made new friends. They were happy.

The next day, the membership applications and up-front payments went crazy. We were now concerned we were getting too many clients. The next day I put in my notice at work. We were amazed to find that it was not only gay people who joined. There were straight people who wanted to come to a place with a friendly vibe, where they could feel free to socialize with their gay friends.

To uphold our reputation in the general community, we decided to draw up rules of conduct. The members were discouraged from displaying erotic, deep kissing or lewd touching in the club. We encouraged affection… light kissing, holding hands and embracing. I remembered my time in the swimming pool with Hong Ge, where we had openly displayed erotic behavior. We didn't want to have guards blowing shrill-whistles in our club or give the cops an excuse to raid us. We warned our clients that if they displayed erotic behavior openly, we would terminate their membership, without refund, and ban them from the club. We also discouraged swearing. We wanted our members to enjoy a place of culture and high standards. There was no porn, no drugs, and a strict dress code.

The men were handsome and smartly dressed, the woman lovely and elegant. We did not encourage more men, or more women. We wanted equal numbers. After all, gay men want to be in the company of women, and gay women in the company of men. It was nice to see lovers holding hands, and not having to look over their shoulders. Their smiling faces gave us all the reward we needed.

It was a good business and there was not much money on the premises. People paid their membership, with their credit card. From this, we also deducted their food and drinks account directly. Then at the end of each month, we sent them a statement.

That very first night, we opened the club, it felt so good. We were elated because our clients were happy, but also because we could tell that it had been good financial decision as well. I was more cautious, but Jinrong was really excited, "If we earn enough, we can travel to all different parts of the world", she told me dreamily.

I smiled at her exuberance. I couldn't help the voice inside my head that told me to remain cautious, 'There is still a lot of work to be done before then,' I warned her, but I was already thinking about babies and a family… that was all I wanted, but after what happened with Liu Jen, I kept quiet.

CHAPTER 16
NOT AGAIN

Six days a week we ran Yuqing's, and rested on Monday's… Every day the club was full. We had more members than we could handle, and we knew that if they all arrived on the same day we would be in trouble. We worked hard and enjoyed what we did. Our clients all loved Yuquin's. Within a short time, we had our first engagement party, for two men who had met on our opening night. We were witnessing *happiness in motion* and how great the power of same-sex love really is.

The club became famous among the local gay community. When people said, "We'll meet you at Yuqing's", everyone knew where it was.

We started off by only opening in the evenings. In time, we opened for the lunch crowd, then they wanted us to open for breakfast on weekends. Our clients came from all walks of life, wealthy, and the not so wealthy, in a constant stream. My idea when I first thought of the club, was that there needed to be a natural place for people to meet and social-ize, and that its existence was needed in the community.

Among our members there was a lesbian couple, Huang Yuxia and Li Siyi. Huang was small and delicate, like a sparrow, creative, and a bit funky. Li Siyi was taller, stately but also delicate, but with a man's haircut and clothes, that looked natural on her. As they were around the same age as Jinrong and myself, and spoke the same slang, we became good friends. We often went to other restaurants with them and enjoyed their company. Li Siyi was the chairperson of an electronics company, and Huang Yuxia was once an employee of that company, working in the research department. They had been together ever since they met.

Li Siyi didn't talk much about her company or the role she played there, to be the chairperson at such a young age, suggested brilliance. When I questioned her about this she told me that her father was the chairman, but he had died. When she was born, China had the one child policy, so there were no brothers to compete with her. Her dad must have been an unusual man of that time. He made sure she had an excellent business education. He sent her to Sydney University, first to get an accounting degree, and then a Masters of Business Administration. From a very young age, he made sure that Li Siyi came and worked for the company between studying.

"Every time I worked there", She said with a smile, "Father would see that I got experience in a different department. By the time I left high school, I had worked in every department in the business".

They came to the club most weekends, depending on Li Siyi's work pressures. After so many months, we had got to know our regular customers. They came for the wine and the good food, but also to taste the love that nourished the hearts of everyone there. I am not only talking about romantic love. Oh yes, there was plenty of that, but we had created a place where the patrons came with their goodwill. New guests made comments about, *the feel* of the place. They would see everyone happily chatting, smiling and laughing, and experience the unrestrained sea of joy, where gay people didn't have to worry about the disapproving eyes of homophobic people.

After being open for eight months, we had already paid off some of our debt. We were well entrenched in our duties, where I did the accounts and admin, and when time permitted, I fussed around here and there. Jinrong, the maître d, welcomed guests, and was the boss of the kitchen. Her side ran so smoothly that she still had time to chat with patron's, "Nihao, William, have you overcome your influenza?" or, "Mary, has your grandson been born yet?" Everybody loved her. I was blessed, and happy to have her in my life.

However, one night after we got home, and were about to go to bed, she seemed quieter than her normal, exuberant self. When I asked her if she was okay, she gave me a funny look, "I'm just tired," She yawned then turned over to sleep.

The next day at work, she came and said that she needed a rest and wanted to go to the local park for some fresh air. She had never done this before, and again I asked her if she was okay. Again she said that she was tired. I told her, "You go, I'll look after everything while you're gone. In fact, it's a good idea that we both take a break once or twice a day". This happened more and more, and even sometimes at night, which was our busiest time. It was then that my eyes started twitching.

I'm observant, and noticed that when Li Siyi and Huang Yuxia came in, Jinrong was always close by, eagerly fussing over them. I also noticed that when they were not there, that was usually when Jinrong was away. I should have been concerned, but I trusted her. I should have paid more attention when the eye-twitching started again, but I told myself they were, 'just coincidences'.

This strange behavior continued for more than two months, then I realized that I had not seen Li Siyi or Huang Yuxia for a while. At the same time, I noticed that Jinrong seemed to be depressed, and a little lost. Mistakes crept into her work, and she was touchy and would not talk to me about this. Still, I made excuses for the two girls thinking that Li Siyi was working hard or that perhaps they needed a rest from our place... and that they would be back soon enough. Later, thinking about it, perhaps I did not want to know what the twitching was telling me – I was scared to face it.

I tried to comfort her, and she tried to respond with affection.

One night, I received a text message from Li Siyi. She asked if we could meet the next night for a chat. Thinking it must be important, I agreed. Then, strangely, she texted another place where she wanted to meet. This was most concerning, but I decided to go with the flow and not ask questions.

I accepted the arrangements, and went to the appointed restaurant. I said nothing to Jinrong and felt guilty about deceiving her, but somehow it felt like the right thing to do, for now.

The next night, at the appointed time, I found the restaurant. Li Siyi was waiting for me at a reserved table. This was the first time I had seen Li Siyi wearing her formal business suite, and assumed she had come straight from work. Although she looked graceful and elegant, I took it as an ominous sign, that I was going to be *dealt with*. Her face was serious and didn't light up with her usual smile, when she saw me. Her arms were folded and body turned away from me. I felt uncomfortable as I sat down. She took a sip of coffee, without offering me any. In a cold voice, she spoke, "How much money do you want? Two hundred thousand... three hundred thousand... for you to immediately leave this town".

I was taken by complete surprise, "What's this about Li Siyi?... What is this talk?"

For a moment she considered me, and in the same cold voice said, "Are you pretending to not know what is going on?"

I was getting angry, and half shouted, "I know I haven't done anything wrong...but you seem to be accusing me of something... what exactly are you talking about, Li Siya... I don't know what's going on".

She cleared her throat, and leaning forward, as if to intimidate me. Her voice echoed across the table, "You must be aware that your Jinrong is having a relationship with my Yuxia?"

"Relationship with Yuxia?" I whispered. So here it was, once again the ugly truth. With all that I had gone through, the deep lying sadness was just one thin layer below my consciousness and I quickly became teary. I was speechless. I scrambled in my bag for a tissue. She scrutinized my spontaneous breakdown. Being the chairperson that she was, she knew how to read people, and she could see that I was not acting. Yet, she did not soften.

Reaching into her own bag, Li Siyi took out an envelope and handed it to me. Whilst I wondered if it was money. I opened the envelope and took out a stack of photos... intimate photos of Jinrong and Yuxia. I got halfway through them and dropped them on the table, unable, or unwilling to see the rest. I could hear my own heartbeat, pounding in my ears, and felt short of breath. My first hope was that the pics were fake, but I knew they were real. Jinrong's strange behavior confirmed this.

I looked at Li Siyi through teary eyes, "How long has this been going on?"

She shrugged, and coldly said, "three or four months".

I leaned back in my chair, too stunned to say anything. She finished her coffee and started to pack up her things, then it occurred to me to ask her, "What were you talking about money... you think I want money from you... Li, we have been good friends, how could you accuse me of such a thing... Go to hell". With that I gathered the photos back into the envelope and went to confront Jinrong.

Back at the club, I composed myself as much as possible, but I was sure the tension in my face would give me away. As I walked in, she was talking to the head chef. I went up to her and asked, "You got a minute?" then headed for the office. Thirty seconds later she came in.

"Shut the door", I demanded. She looked at me, scared, sensing that I knew. Her face pale.

I was calculating when I asked her, "How are you feeling these days my love? Less tired?" She just looked at me, dumbstruck. So I continued, "Do you need to go for a walk in the park to clear your head? Talk to me... now, where is that *farm girl* ... all that innocence and honesty that was always a mark of your character? Is it still there... seems not". Her eyes got bigger and bigger, but still she was unable to say anything. "What's wrong Jinrong, I have never known you to be so quiet ... feeling guilty perhaps?"

She stammered, "Mu... Muro.... Murong, Wha... What are you talking about? Don't hurt me like this".

I said nothing at first. My heart was crumbling as I stared at the woman I loved but regained my composure, "So, everything is just perfect in your world, you haven't been doing anything naughty behind my back, have you?"

She began to cry, and silently pleading with me to stop. I took the photos out of my bag, slowly removing them from the envelope, and dropping them on the desk. I did not trust myself to say anything else. I watched as she pathetically picked them up, and after seeing the first one, the muscles of her hand weakened, they dropped to the floor, mostly face up, reflecting the brutal truth. In shock, we both stared blankly at the images. I lay my head on the desk, broken. She was sobbing. We ignored the ringing phone… pretending not hear the knocks on the office door. Our world, together had just ended.

Finally she mumbled, "I got it wrong, Murong… please…. please forgive me". My head remained on the desk, unable to move, or speak as the resentment welled inside. I remember thinking, 'I hate that I love so much', but shouted, "Betrayed, you betrayed me… deceived me… broke the most important sacrament that two people can have between them… robbed me of the one thing that kept me going, putting my trust into you. You, who should have known better than to belittle the trust between us. You are no better than any man".

The grief I felt over the loss of Yuqing besieged me, the insult of Liu Jen's weakness cut into me. At least Hong Ge had been honest about his infidelity. I lay there, a mix of sadness, anger and self-doubt. Life had, once more, played an evil trick on me. Now the anger rose up inside of me. It took me over… it took me by surprise. I jumped up and slapped Jinrong hard across the face. I grabbed her by the hair and pulled her head back with it, and kept on slapping her in the face. She stood there, not fighting back, as if she deserved the punishment, as if it would purge her somehow.

In that moment, I hated every part of her, but I also hated what I was doing to her... it wasn't going to solve anything... the damage was done. I slumped back into my chair, ashamed. Looking up at her tear stained face I could see the hurt I had inflicted on her... scratches... red blotches... there would be bruises. I felt like a demon. There was no excuse for the violence that had erupted inside of me.

I took a deep breath. My voice came out in a whisper, "Jinrong, I am sorry... I am sorry for attacking you..." With that I walked out of the Yuqing Club, and never looked back.

CHAPTER 17
SELF-HURT

I went home, filled my daypack with a few things, and took some cash. I scribbled a note to Jinrong telling her she could have the club. I told her that the debt was now her responsibility and all I wanted was the money I originally invested. I told her to never contact me again. Sarcastically, I told her to have a nice life with Yuxia. They were both cheats, who deserved each other. I slung my daypack over my shoulder and walked out. I had taken a hand full of sedatives, which now made me feel like a crazed person... I was out of my head. I was broken and hardly noticed the rain pelting down as I aimlessly walked the streets. It didn't matter that I was cold... icy self-pity clutched at my heart. I wandered the streets like a homeless beggar that has nowhere else to go, no responsibility.

Enzo was sitting hunched over, his head in his hands thinking, "How much can one young woman take in such a short lifetime?" He sat up and searched her young face... it was expressionless. He thought of how he had found her on that windy day ... a broken and weather beaten girl, standing on a bridge ready to leap to her death. He offered her more tea, but Murong shook her head. She wanted to continue. It was comforting to have somebody listen to her, without judgment.

"I have experienced so many hardships over the years. My heart has been bruised and battered. I believed that women would be more reliable than men, that she was more trustworthy. I didn't expect Life to torment me again. But you know what is horrible"? She asked Enzo.

"What?"

"It is never being able to trust another person again... what sort of life is that? I trusted her, I trusted Liu Jen, I trusted Hong Ge, and I trusted my time with Yuqing would last forever... I lost trust and hope in my parents to support me. So the worst thing is that I can't even trust myself to make wise decisions or be blessed with a good life. I have no faith in anyone anymore... I have lost faith in God, and I have no faith in myself."

He started to say 'Murong," but she cut him off.

"I didn't want the gay club. I didn't the money. I only wanted eternal quiet and peace... I should have jumped before you came. My heart is dead. There is no life worth talking about. I dragged my body around the streets, sleeping with the destitute and homeless. I have no soul.... like a zombie... a ghost of ghosts. There is no place in this world for me... I hate myself and I wanted to harm myself because that's all I think I deserve.

One night, I passed the door of a club. I glanced in and saw some woman who were scantily dressed. They were all drunk and shouting and laughing with some men. I knew very well what they were doing. How could I look down on them, as really, I was one of them? In a heavy mood I went in and asked where the boss was. One girl pointed to a door.

I went to the door, and knocked, "What?" shouted a male voice. I entered the room, where there was a fat slob of a man of about fifty years old, wearing a beach suit, sunglasses on his forehead, with a cigar clenched in his teeth. When he saw me, he gestured for me to sit down. Slowly he took off his sunglasses, gently lowered the cigar, and sucked in his lips for a moment.

"I want to be a prostitute". I said.

"Have you done this before?"

I shook my head, but said, "I know enough".

"Stand up", he said, "turn around". He whistled. Then said, "I always test the girls. Are you willing?"

I looked him in the eye, as I started to undo my jacket buttons. I let everything fall to the floor. He just watched me. He pulled the curtains closed and made sure the door was locked. He undid his belt and let his pants drop to the floor. He opened his top draw and pulled out a condom, and passed it to me, "Put this on". I did and kept my eyes on his the entire time. I did not hurry. Once it was on, he pushed me over his desk, face downwards. He entered me from behind, whilst he pushed me into the desk. With slow, regular thrusts I could feel him getting closer to climax, his penis thickening as it was about to happen. My heart was a mess. I hated Jinrong and all the others for betraying me. I knew what I was doing to myself was disgusting, but I needed self-punishment. I shouted at him, "Deeper... harder". He ignored me. He knew what he was doing... very professional, until he came, and as he did he pushed it in further as he shuddered with sensitivity.

Afterwards, we dressed, but he kept watching my face, then said, "With your body and appearance, your light colored skin, plus your cheeky way, you can be a five-level girl. You could probably build up to around 200 tricks a month, then we will assess how you progress. Maybe, we can upgrade you to seven hundred.

I smiled and asked him what I would be earning. It was an act, but one I needed to do. I did not care about the money. If life treated me the way it did, then I was going to treat myself and life with the same disrespect.

He gave me a plastic vial of tablets, "Take these so you don't get pregnant. You will live here... ask the other girls where all the clothes are, dress elegantly, and with your shape men will flock to you. Start off slowly, and ease into it. I don't want you to burnout within the first month. You get fifteen percent of what you collect. Your food and lodging will be taken care of. Now go, and find Haung. Tell her that she must put you on the books. She will show you the ropes.

I walked out of the office calmly, glancing around me. I saw a young male waiter. I smiled at him. He knew what I had just done, and seemed a little nervous. I noticed a smart looking, middle aged woman, wearing Western style clothing. I went up to her and asked if she was by any chance, Haung, "Yes, are you a new girl?" I nodded as she appraised me. She continued, "You get your instructions from me. If you behave well, we will get on well, but remember with so many girls here there is no special treatment".

She showed me the cubicle that I would now call home. It was tiny but clean. She showed me the bathroom down the hall, then the ladies lounge, which was our private rest and social area. Guests were not allowed in there. It was about seventy-square-meters, and friendly enough, with sofas, TVs, coffee machine, books in book shelves, etc. I learned that there were around sixty girls who worked there. But mostly it was empty as the girls were usually *'working'*.

The guest areas were luxurious. There were five floors in total, each covering an area of about 300 square meters. Each floor had a number of deluxe suites with brown-red leather sofas and mahogany floors below. On the walls, were new, large LCD screens, with JBL speakers. Models walking the catwalk were on display for the customers to watch. There were also a variety of sensual massage rooms and guest bedrooms, which were equally luxurious.

CHAPTER 18
AND SO THE MEN CAME

After advice and help from some of the other girls who had been working there for a long time, I had my first floor experience the next day. I had dressed the part, and within ten minutes of being in the guest lounge I was bought a drink. Generally we would stand around and the customers would buy us a drink. By doing so, they thought they could grab and handle us, with lecherous behavior. At first I cringed, but self-harming as I was, I endured it. After all, they are not likely to *'rent'* you if you are offish.

A week later, I was told that I was ready to start working. We were to entertain a group of business men, in a private lounge. There were six girls, and six men. Food and the drinks kept rolling in, and Haung made sure it was all well organized. It was not long before the boss of the group started to feel me up. He had clearly picked me. He was in his forties, and physically fit, a big man... his shirt tight on his chest and shoulders. It was not long before the pretense of business conversation dried up, and each man put his focus on the girl he had chosen. I felt uncomfortable. It all seemed dreamlike, but we are still laughing, eating and drinking while the man had me open his fly and fondle him.

Each couple had their own private bedroom, and the two of us slipped into ours. He closed the door. Sexily, I started to take off my clothes, while he sat back and enjoyed the performance. Just as slowly, he then took off his clothes. As I expected, he had thick arms, shoulders, and a strong six-pack. He was at least 400mm taller than me. His erection was red and hard. My mood was still a dreamscape – a mixture of excitement and fear.

He lay me quietly on the bed, opened my legs, and climbed on top of me. I was hoping for foreplay, to get me ready, but he jammed it in. Being the big man that he was, as he lay on me with his full weight, I felt like I was being squashed into the sheets. He pumped harder and faster, deeper and deeper, but I did not let on that it was hurting. As he came, it was my duty to pretend that he has stimulated me so much that I also came with him. I acted this part well. I thought he was finished, but he kept going... this position, then that. At one stage he put his penis in my mouth and worked my head back and forth. After about two hours, his battery began to run low and finally he rolled off, finished. After another glass of whiskey, he fell asleep. I am sure his snoring was heard all the way down the hall.

I was not sleepy, so got up and had a shower. Wrapping a silk dressing gown around me, I went to the balcony to pass the time. The scenery was busy, people threading their way through the congested traffic of the narrow street... people going about their day's work. Men and women with large wooden wheel barrows were carrying fruit and goods up and down the street, business men, with brief cases strutted past to show how important they were. As I watched all these people doing their daily work, one old lady must have sensed that I was looking down, she looked up at me. I wondered if she was thinking the same thing, 'there is that young girl, doing her daily work'. I smiled to myself at the thought.

After some two hours of sex with that man, I was still horny. He simply did not satisfy me because of his own selfish needs. I occasionally enjoy smoking and so lit a cigarette and looked at the bustling streets below. I enjoyed the scene, and it gave me a sense of connection to fellow humans, away from that *animal* snoring inside.

It was getting dark and the red lanterns and neon's gave it a feeling of warmth. I took a deep breath to try and calm myself down. Could I really handle what just happened 10 000 times or more into the future? I shuddered at the thought. Then I heard him shout, "Girl, come…come and make me feel good".

I went inside, not really knowing why I was subjecting myself to this. Perhaps by doing so I was dying some more inside, moving ever closer to self-annihilation. Perhaps, it is just my way of dealing with the screwed up emotions that were circulating within me – after all, I was not cutting bits out of my skin, or drinking myself into oblivion.

From that day, I received guests almost every day. Sometimes in the quieter times, the girls and I would chat or play cards. I liked them. They were all doing the best they could for the life they had. The smart ones saved their money and didn't do drugs or alcohol. They use to say, "I am riding a donkey so one day I can ride a horse". Some of them were fools, who just blew their money. They didn't think about the future, when their looks will be gone and management asks them to leave. Once on the streets, they will descend into oblivion, and most will be dead within a few years.

There was no sexual pleasure in receiving my clients. I could have been an actor on the stage, playing a part. It was one faceless, leering man, after the other... a collision of the flesh in a vague, foggy reality.

I wondered if this was a psychological method we humans use to protect us from being damaged by traumatic experiences, much the same as we sometimes block out the memory of horrible events. 'This is good', I told myself, 'I do not want to remember these men, this army of men, when I am old...if I get old'. No matter how many I serviced, there were thousands more. They came in all shapes and sizes... different guises, young, middle-aged and old, belligerent, needy. Occasionally three or four would take me at the same time. Still, I am never sexually satisfied. These men do not bring me to orgasm. S and M would happen occasionally but they had to pay management extra for kinky extras. I never allowed this for myself. I told Haung, if she made me do that, I would leave. They knew that I was too much of an asset to let go of me. Some of the other girls were not as strong, and I would hear their screams and see the bruises and cuts on their bodies the next day.

We woman were like cattle, being paraded at a market, and that is how the men treated us. I endured this because its pain and disrespect helped me to forget the pain of my past. When it was quiet, we were allowed to go out to a restaurant or for a drink. As we walked the streets, we could feel the cold stares of those who judged us. They would spit at our feet and condemn us. I wanted to say to them that it was their men that were keeping us employed, and in my opinion, their men were not even as good as animals. Yet, there were some men who would just come to talk. They were scared, like me... men who were prepared to pay for a half hour chat. It got them out of their lonely lives, where I was more like a loving daughter to them. They would leave feeling better. I also felt better for helping them – the offering of a little bit of respect.

CHAPTER 19
MORE SELF-HURT

Over time I got to know most of the girls. We were sisters in an industry of shame and pain. We all understood it was a necessary industry. When we were resting, chatting, or just surfing the net, in our private lounge we were all just normal girls … young girls roaming around in pajamas and large slippers. One of them wore a pajama top with a big cartoon mouse. Behind the scenes there were no sexy clothes or bright lipstick, no standing tall, as they slopped around, like normal girls would do at home. Some had teddy bears or floppy puppies on their beds.

Although we all came from different parts of the country, we all had similar stories, all been ravaged by life. The smart one's were already planning to open a shop, selling anything but sex. In the lounge we were a fraternity where we supported each other after a brutal client, or some emotional breakdown. Together, we knew that we are human beings, not animals. We all had our own stories, and our own need for self-respect, when we allowed it to emerge, but for many it never did. Our wounds and our pains were only known to us.

The only sexual pleasure that we girls got was when we gave it to ourselves. Most nights, a girl would curl up with a girl.

It was there that we were held with compassion, and we gave back with equal compassion. We heard girls whispering and pleasuring each other. These times made the rest bearable. Many girls stayed as partners whilst in that place, and most were loyal within that relationship.

One night, after a man I had been with, lay back on the pillows, grinning with satisfaction and lighting a cigarette, said to me, "That was as good as the first time. Do you remember?"

I didn't remember any man unless they brutalized me, but said politely, "Of course... you know how to satisfy a woman".

He placed a hand on my leg and said, "If you had a good time, why not get out of this place, and become my mistress?"

It made me feel nervous. I did not think it would be good to be owned by one man... it was dangerous. Yet, I had been thinking that it was time to leave. He noticed my hesitation, stuffed the cigarette out in the ashtray on the bed, and touched my head gently, "If you are my lover, you'll live in a beautiful villa. You will also receive 5,000RMB a month. It will be a luxurious life, fine clothes and food. There won't be a million different men, just me. How about it? I will give you a week to consider". He gave me a business card and left.

The next day, there were not many guests, and I studied the business card. He was, Chuxing, the CFO of a property group. I searched the net and saw that they were a massive company, with properties all over the country. Their head office was in Dongguan. It did not surprise me. I could tell that he was rich.

I asked some of the girls to inquire about Chuxing. It seemed that he had been a frequent visitor there – he liked woman with good sized and firm breasts, as well as a light skinned body. There was talk that he was connected to the underworld, and so people were afraid to say much. Some of the girls said that that I was better off staying, but others said it could be a blessing, so I should grab the opportunity. I weighed up all my options as I considered the proposition. Yes, it would be risky, but I was tired of the constant stream of men. I thought it would be good to live in luxury and serve just one man. I sent him a text message, and said yes to being exclusively his lover.

He arrived a few days later and hired me as usual. Perhaps he was double checking that he had made the right choice. Afterwards, he said, "Are you packed? I've come to take you away from here".

His BMW 7 Series was parked outside with a driver. He told the driver to go to his villa in Fenggang. Only the very wealthy could live in this upmarket suburb. It was a lovely area. There are about 300 Greek Style villas on the estate, all with white walls and brown roofs, a bit like an old Christian church, but more modern and elegant. They are all perched on the hillside with beautiful views of green landscapes. The place felt warm and romantic, but I knew that this man was not a romantic. I was his *play thing*, and I would only last as long as he was entertained by me.

The driver pulled up and parked outside one villa that had a good view of the area. He got my bag from the boot and went inside, whilst Chuxing showed me around the garden. He instructed the driver to show me around the villa and settle me into my bedroom, much the same as a bell boy would show a hotel guest their room, in a very formal way. It was then that I got the sense that I had made a mistake.

The villa was three-stories. The top floor was his penthouse for when he stayed over. The entrance lobby had a rich red carpet. There was a large brown-red timber staircase, with a carved balustrade. It was opulent, like a glossy magazine advert. I wondered if I was dreaming. Everything was modern and expensive.

He asked, "Do you like it?" I had to say yes, like I was star-struck, but I knew that this is just an illusion. I was just a poor guest at his whim and fancy. I had no doubt, he had countless woman there before me, and I was just his latest. He smiled and kissed me on the lips, and put his hand into my shirt. He twiddled my nipple like it was a dial on an old radio.

He showed me the key rack, and took off two keys. "This one is the front door key. This other, is for the Toyota in the garage. You are welcome to use it". He gave me the mobile number of the driver and said if I needed anything important for the villa or if there was a problem I must call him and he will organize it, I was not to bother him with trivial matters. He told me the cleaners come in three times a week, so I needn't do any housework.

Then off he went with the driver. He did not say when he was returning. Nor did I ask.

'Well, now, a high class hooker,' I thought to myself, 'I might as well make the best of it'. I went to my room to unpack my few, pathetic items. I didn't really need any of them. The walk-in wardrobe was stocked with beautiful clothes, all the perfect size. I wondered how he picked these for me, or if all his girls had the same body type.

I undressed and soaked in a large spar bath. There were oils and scented candles. I felt like a princess as my tired body relaxed and my inner self felt rejuvenated. I lay there for at least an hour, relaxed and calm. I gently fondled myself until I came. I had no idea what the end result would be of my decision to go to this villa, to become a kept woman. Over the years my life had been a series of changing snap shots – here, there, and all over the place, with different faces. I knew that this was a temporary place, but I decided I would make the most of it.

CHAPTER 20
BAD, BAD CHOICE

I lived alone there. Day and night I was mostly alone. The cleaners would come and go. The driver dropped off shopping bags with food and toiletries, but he kept to himself and said very little. Chuxing came to me to play, and I fulfilled my role. Sometimes he was only there for ten minutes. Occasionally, he stayed overnight, alone in hid pent house. He had another life and I was not given any of it. There was one time where I had to accompany him to a business lunch. He sent me to have my hair done and I had to dress like royalty. I had to look my best and sound intelligent – he seemed pleased.

Most of the time, he only arrived at night and stayed for a little while.

Sometimes I would drive to the fashionable side of town and go clothes shopping in the best boutiques. I was always fragrant and spicy for him, and had to be ready, as I never knew when he would pop in. When he came to visit overnight, the driver had a small room outside where he watched TV or slept. I did get lonely sometimes but I was enjoying my life. I spent a lot of my time reading, surfing the net, calling my friends, and the days and weeks just flew by. I tried not to think about my past… what Jinrong did to me, and all the other painful events. I wanted to focus only on one day at a time… live in the now. Up until now, my life had been hard work, and now I was enjoying the physical and sensory stimulation, even though it was a *fool's paradise*. I was no longer scared, I had nothing to lose, and with the use of a car, I had freedom. I was living for myself.

As the months passed, he became less friendly, bossier, and more demanding with the sex. On occasions when he left I was bruised and sore. He started to want more S & M and he got a thrill from belittling and hurting me. I adjusted and said nothing. I was a prostitute of body and mind, and he owned me to do with me what pleased him. I also wondered if his business enterprises were not going well as he seemed worried and anxious a lot of the time, but I did not ask. I just tried to please him. In my mind it was simple… sleep with him…make him happy, bank the money, and enjoy the luxury the rest of the time when he was away.

One night, it was raining heavily, and I thought he would not come, but then I heard the sound of his car enter the garage. I heard him say something to the driver, then his footsteps up the stairs. I quickly checked my hair and smoothed down my blouse and skirt and was at the door to greet him. He just brushed passed me, and as he did I could smell strong cigarette smoke and alcohol on his clothes and body. There was also the heavy smell of cologne. He was drunk, and surly. I helped him take off his coat and tie. He immediately grabbed me hard between the legs and squeezed, like one would squeeze a pair of pliers. His eyes were glazed, and as he scrutinized my face as he squeezed harder. I could not help but wince, but said nothing, until he pushed me away, so he could go and fix himself a drink.

My eyes started twitching, but I had no time to consider this as he ordered me to get the belt and handcuffs. When I came back and stood in front of him he grabbed my blouse and ripped it open, buttons flew in all directions. His smile scared me as he literally tore my clothes off. My underpants were pulled so hard they ripped in half. When I was naked he leered at me has he took off his clothes. He grabbed his erection and fondled himself.

I tried to reason with him, and said "Chuxing you are drunk. Please don't hurt me". He scoffed, "I own you, like I own a dog... and I will do with you as I please". He turned me around and placed me in the handcuffs, then pushed me hard on the bed. With the belt he whipped my backside. I quickly turned around, facing him. He then bent down and savagely bit a breast. There was no blood, but deep red teeth marks. He went to the sideboard and drank his whiskey and poured another. Drunkenly, he said, "Murong, you are going to enjoy this whether you like it or not".

As he came back I tried to squirm away, but he grabbed me by a leg and pulled me back to him. "Yes, try and squirm away, I like that".

I'm sure my eyes were wide with fear, and he seemed to be enjoying it. As he raised the belt, I closed my eyes, but this did not stop the pain as it hit my breasts and stomach. He laughed and did it again. I heard myself plead, "No... no, please... don't", but I could tell from his eyes that that was exactly what he wanted.

The next hour or was a blur in the agony, of crying, whimpering, pleading. At one stage, when he was inside me, he leaned back, and punched me in the stomach, and as I recoiled over in pain, he ejaculated. In the end, my body hurt all over, and my skin was red hot with bruises, welts and cuts. All the while, the thunder and heavy rain outside would have muffled my screams, as if Life bought the wrath of the heavens on top of me for my sins.

When he had gone, I called some of the girls from the club to come and help me to get to hospital. They looked shocked when they saw my ravaged, naked body. Silently, they looked with horror, from one to the other. I remained in hospital for two days, in too much pain to move. Later, one of the girl's told me that the day before he had beaten one of the new girl's at KTV. She was so badly beaten that he was banned from the place, and told that he would be beaten up if he showed his face there again. I wondered why this man had developed such a need to cause suffering to another human being as he did. Or, why be in a relationship where he cared absolutely nothing about the emotional and sexual needs of his partner.

I never returned to the villa. The girls made sure that they packed my bag and got the money I had. I begged them not to steal anything as I did not want reprisals. After the hospital, I stayed with an aunt of one of the girls. This was in the countryside and I felt safe. I paid her board and lodging, as they were very poor.

Over the months I was there, I recovered in mind and body. Once again, I considered my future. There were times when I wished he had gone that little bit further and actually killed me, but no, that would have been too easy.

CHAPTER 21
LIFE AGAIN?

I couldn't help but wonder why my whole life had been so desperate. I even thought that maybe when my parents gave birth to me, it was a mistake. It was punishment after punishment. There was no point of living, other than pain… physical and emotional pain.

After three months I knew I had to leave the aunt's house as there was not really enough room for us all, and I felt in the way. I bid her and her family farewell and headed back to the city, where I would become one of the lost millions again.

After a month on the streets, out in the weather, with nothing but misery, I decided to end my life. So on a cool morning, when the weak sun was making a mockery of the morning light, I stood on the Haiyin Bridge, looking down at the swirling water of Pearl River in Guangzhou.

I was calm, and felt no remorse. I thought about my family briefly, and scoffed at the thought of them being concerned about whether I was alive or dead. They would continue without me as they had done for years. My life was an endless conveyor belt of anguish and pain – it was now time to get off it. I was tired of trying …there was no more trying left within me. A part of me felt proud of the resilience I had shown over the years to keep bouncing back, but all it had led me to, was more of the same. I was not sad. In fact, I felt relief and felt like I was doing what was required of me. Death would release it all.

Looking down on that wide grey river, far below, I was in no hurry, as death would be forever. I moved forward in determined preparation, I was looking forward to the prospect of the darkness soon to come. I closed my eyes gently, and with a smile on my lips took that small step forward. I fell freely in the air for a few seconds until slamming into the river. The cold assaulted me, but I knew the cold would help me to go faster. I relaxed into its clutches. All my life I had been controlled by the flow of events. Now, in this river's embrace, I let its flow take me as it wanted, to my end. It wouldn't take long for hyperthermia to set in, leading to unconsciousness... my lungs would fill with water... then I would drown.

My life flashed through my mind and I let the images pass without nostalgia, as my soul packed it bags to leave me. As it flashed by, I realized that I had added to the lives of just about everyone who I had come in contact with. This pleased me. I started shivering, my breathing became labored, I was going... It was pleasant, my body drifting under water and slowly turning... then nothing.

I woke up on the side of the river, coughing water, and felt someone pumping my chest, applying CPR on me. 'Damn,'

is all I could think. When I coughed water and opened my eyes, I saw a young man kneeling next to me. I heard him say, "Thank God… you are alive".

I thought, 'damn' again, but the coughing of the water took all my energy, as I vomited up what seemed to be buckets of it. Other than that, my mind was blank, but I knew that I could do this again, and next time it would be at 2.00 am when all was quiet and nobody would see me. I fell back into unconsciousness. I woke up in another hospital. The same young guy was sitting next to my bed.

Noticing that I was awake, he asked my name. He went to call a nurse. She came in, took my pulse, and checked my vital signs. She smiled, and said, "Lucky you, all is perfectly well". I think, 'shit'. Still smiling she continued, "The doctor wants to keep you in for a few more hours as a precaution". She left and went to the nurse's desk.

The young man was smiling, looking proud of himself for saving me. I didn't say anything, just closed my eyes. I was a zombie, I was alive, shivering, but I wanted to be dead, 'Thanks'.

He asked, "How are you feeling?"

I said nothing, but thought 'Grrrrrrrrrrrrr'.

"My name is Lai Jintao. I saw you jump into the river, and so ran down the river and jumped in after you".

"Why? I don't want to live, you fool. Did you not realize that?"

Hearding this, he was despondent for a few seconds, looking at me with a silly expression on his face. For a moment he said nothing, and with a teasing expression continued, "Oh, so you want to die? Well I can take you back to the river and push you back in… or perhaps I can throttle you here and now in the bed". Normally I would have laughed at this but in that moment not much was funny.

He leaned towards me, and in a confidential whisper said, "I told the paramedics that you were looking at the water, and slipped in. If I had said you tried to commit suicide, they would treat you as a loony, and you would have to go to the psych ward… and that wouldn't be much fun, so when the doctor asks you, say you saw a photo floating in the river and you were curious and slipped in".

"Thanks, that was smart of you".

He asked if I had any friends I wanted to go to when I was discharged. I said no. He sat for a few minutes, then apologized that he needed to go home for a shower, as he was also cold, and to change into dry clothes. He would be back in a few hours and would help me out of the hospital.

I dozed most of that time and woke up with him sitting next to the bed. He was reading some sort of text book. When he saw I was awake he closed his book and smiled.

For the first time I really looked at him, 'Not much more than an adolescent', I thought. He had strong, dark eyebrows with clear skin. His features were well chiseled, an interesting face. He was slightly built, almost petite like a young girl. I guessed he was around seventeen but later learnt that he was twenty-one.

I was stunned by this small young man, and wondered how he could swim in and drag me to the shore against the fast flowing river. I asked him what he was reading and he said he was studying writing, as he wanted to write stories. We chatted for about ten minutes before a doctor came in and checked on me. Reading my chart, the doctor said, "So how did you end up in the river Miss?" I think he was double checking that it wasn't an attempted suicide. I rattled off the story Jintao had made up. The doctor said, "As you seem fine, you can be discharged. Next time though, don't go so close to the water's edge".

Jintao waited for the doctor to be far enough away and let out a suppressed giggle. I did the same. He asked me, "So, where are you going... can I help you to go there?"

"No thanks, I'll be okay to be left alone".

Shaking his head, "Uhh Uh, not a chance... You threatened earlier that you would head straight back to the river".

"Go, I don't want you around", I replied irritably.

He was thoughtful, then challenged me in a way I did not expect. "Either, you let me take you to some of your friends, or I will go and tell that doctor that we both lied and that you tried to kill yourself... so, what is it to be?"

I nodded, "Okay, so you blackmail me... Can we go somewhere and talk? I'm hungry, but if we do, promise you will not ask me why I jumped into the river". He agreed.

The nurse returned with my clothes, freshly laundered, and the money and my credit card that had been in my pocket, folded, neatly on top.

He left the ward as I dressed and met me at the nurse's desk for me to check out. He said that there was a small family restaurant across the road, so we headed there.

Once we sat down, he seemed less talkative, and even a little nervous. I realized that in the hospital, with me stuck in bed, he was more self assured, but now alone with me he was shy, as if he had never been with a girl before.

"Are you nervous being alone with me?' I asked him, staring into his face, with a self-deprecating smile, "Probably because I am not used to being around women. In the past, there were few girls in high school but I was always shy, so I have not had much experience with women, and with China's one child policy, I didn't have a sister to teach me. I'm sorry if I seem a bit stupid in this way".

I reassured him that he was doing fine, but thought to myself that the poor boy was probably still a virgin. This was a funny, and very awkward boy but there was also something charming and kind about him.

As we drank tea, we chatted about this and that, "What do you do when you're not fishing ladies out of the river... are you a student?"

'No, not anymore, I recently graduated from college. I studied IT, but majored in mobile software.... I'm just an entry-level programmer in a company". There was a moment of silence so I asked, "You like writing?"

"I love writing stories...fiction books in my spare time."

"Wow", I said impressed. "Where do you live?"

"About ten minutes away, not far. I have a tiny apartment. I live alone."

He was quiet for a moment, and asked, "Once you've eaten, where can I take you? I work funny hours and will be on duty tonight so I have some time free now".

"I have no home... nowhere to go..."

"You must have somewhere... some friends?"

"Nope, I don't. I could find friends to stay with but I don't want to... as you kept me alive, if I am to try again, I need a fresh start... you could take me to your place?"

He looked shocked, "I can't, it's too small", but I think he was just scared of being alone with a girl. Now it was my turn to blackmail him, "Either you let me stay at your place for a while, or I go back to the river... it's up to you".

Again he surprised me when he said, "I can cook for you. I love cooking".

'Eh?' I thought.

He continued, "The unit is not very good, and really small. It's all I can afford".

I noticed he avoided looking directly at me. "I don't care if it's a hole in the ground. I have been living on the streets, and as long as it's dry and clean, I don't mind... maybe we can try it for a time, and see what happens." I started to tease him, "I could be your girlfriend."

Spontaneously he burst out, "Really," then, with a bit more composure, "are you serious? I... I... need to know so I don't make a fool of myself."

I gave his arm a light punch, "Who knows the reason why you fished me out of that river."

"Yeah, I go fishing... don't catch a fish... I catch a girl...." Looking downwards, embarrassed, he said coyly, "You will have to teach me about girls".

When I heard that, I admired his honesty. "Well, you saved my life I am now your responsibility. If you don't want me, you must carry me back to the river and throw me in," then I added, a bit more seriously, "I can pay my way. I have money in a bank account, so it won't cost you anything ... so that's settled then... let's stop talking and order some food. I'm starving". He shook his head, and smiled at me, as if to say he couldn't believe what had just happened to him. We both opened our menus, and decided what to eat.

CHAPTER 22
THE LIGHT SHINES

His rental unit, was a double-decker, with a tiny bedroom space on a mezzanine floor. The lower area was an open plan kitchen, lounge, and dining room. It had a small folding table, three plastic stools, and some simple appliances, and not much room for anything else. The bathroom adjoined this room and was just big enough for the toilet and shower. It was quiet, and I was happy to see that he kept it clean and tidy. He was a bit embarrassed about how basic it was. I assured him, that I had been living in worse conditions. I didn't tell him about the luxury villa that I had recently abandoned. I didn't want him to feel intimidated by my history.

He put the kettle on and offered me tea. He had all the traditional teas of China... green tea, yellow tea, Oolong, Pu'er and black tea. We had Oolong.

As we sipped on our tea, I said to him, "We will take our time to make love... not today... maybe not tomorrow. You see, making love is like making this tea. There should be a ceremony, and it takes time to mature... it's a language, not an act. I will show you a little bit each day... so young man, don't be in a hurry." I could see he was relieved by this. He was probably nervous that he would have to perform tonight.

An hour later Jintao went to work, but he said it was only a short shift and that he will be back about 2.00 am. I gave him a quick kiss on the cheek, and pushed him out the door. As he went down the corridor, he was still shaking his head in disbelief.

That eventful morning, jumping into the river, in hope that I would end my world, had taken its toll on my emotions. I was tired and drained, so I lay down on the bed and instantly feel asleep. When I woke up, I familiarized myself with the apartment. I made a list of things I thought we needed. Other than an entire cupboard of herbs and spices, there was very little food. I went down to the local supermarket, just on the opposite corner of the street. When I got back I cooked us a wholesome meal for when he got home.

As only he knew I was there, it was a liberating thought, being hidden! This was just what I needed.

He said I was welcome to use his PC to play games or surf the net if I wanted. I checked my emails and sat playing some games until I heard his key in the door, just after 2.00 am. He came tiptoeing in so as not to wake me if I was asleep. When he saw me awake, he grinned, "I smell something delicious in the kitchen".

I went over to him and gave him a hug of gratitude, "I hope you like it. I thought you would be hungry".

"So, you waited up for me?"

"Yep, but I did have a nap just after you left. Hurry, go and clean up so I can dish up".

When he came out of the bathroom he was showered and clean. Then with great interest he said, "That really smells good".

"Just something a friend once taught me", I said with a smile.

He dipped his fork into the bowl, and began turning it all over, whilst he sniffed. I was about to complain, thinking my food wasn't good enough, but then he said surprised, "Zhanjiang ... this food is from Zhanjiang, I like this food."

I was stunned, "How on earth did you know that?" "I told you, I love food... in fact cooking is my hobby. Instead of running around looking for girls, I stay at home and cook".

I plonked on the chair, and my jaw must have touched my knees. He laughed, "Why do you find this so amazing... I have always loved cooking". His face lit up when he spoke about food and all his previous shyness seemed to evaporate.

I recovered and said, "That's wonderful. I hope it's as good as it smells".

The food was good, and he agreed it was delicious. We chatted and joked our way through the meal. He was becoming more relaxed. He kept smiling, and said, "You being here, and this food, I can't tell you how happy I am. Food is the only thing that brings joy into my life. Otherwise, I get lonely, I don't really like my job, but I do it because I need the money".

After we cleaned up we got into bed together. His first lesson was to just be held, in the spoon position. I told him, his erection must go down and we will sleep holding each other, and when I turn over, so must he. We chatted and finally slept. I taught him that making love was not just a physical act. It was about all the things that go in between, like the way we greet each other in the morning, and that it wasn't just about genitalia and orgasm. He was intrigued to learn that orgasm was really only a small part of making love… that the eyes, and how they look at each other, and really see each other was also important. It was about the small things we did to support each other, the affection, and the gestures, that were all part of foreplay. It was about talking and being totally present with each other, the listening and hearing, and above all, it was about always being authentic.

His parents were school teachers and he was an only child. They had instilled in their son, ethics and respect for other people. Their genuine love for each other had shown him that it was natural and easy to love another. The *puppy love* he felt for me, developed into something much more, over time, and I could not help but be affected by his natural ways and sense of humor. I looked forward to spending more and more time with him.

The days turned to weeks. The sex and love were good. I often walked the streets when he worked, and chatted to the people I passed. We became friends. I realized that I was happy. My love for him was not from the flesh, but from the heart. There were no burdens in my heart, and there was never any sense of guilt. Everything was calm and our love came naturally to us.

He introduced me to delicious dishes, one by one. The first dish he cooked was from the Hakka Nationality, and was called, 'Three Cups of Chicken'. The Hakka people are made up of the Han nationality. He explained that his uncle is a Hakka, and it was he who had introduced him to this food. The food reminded him of his uncle, and so was one of his favorite flavors.

Over time, little by little, I told him about my past. His attention was complete, and at times he got angry, with some of the people and how they had treated me. Not once did he judge me. With genuine indignity, said, "Who is this man?" referring to my time in the villa. "This scum is far below your level... you deserved much better". I was secretly pleased that he was angry on my behalf. When I told him of my abortion, he had tears in his eyes. I held him tight until he calmed down.

He had saved my life when he fished me out of that river, and now he was saving my soul with his love for me. It was a pleasure and an honor to be his girlfriend.

There is an ancient Chinese saying, *When I reported it to Yongquan, I always have the grace to repay my enemies* (Yongquan mean's fountain, so the adage mean's – if you give me a drop of water, then I will return it to the fountain, and therefore be thankful). My need to self-harm was gone, and I was in a much better frame of mind to give and receive love and happiness.

CHAPTER 23
REDEMPTION

Happy days drifted to become happier months and life was easy. Yet, I couldn't help be anxious on occasions. After all, something had destroyed every relationship that I had been in.

In Jintao's spare time, he would prepare stunning meals or was at his computer writing. I would read and relax, or study different things, such as dressmaking, or flower arranging. My favorite though, was studying classical Chinese characters. I spent hours at the table with my special maobi pen (a traditional pen made with horsehair, so the characters can flow), or I would read his stories and help him with ideas. Because he did not enjoy his job, and because he was industrious, I wanted to help him, but said nothing because he often said that it was the man's responsibility to make the household money, and not take it from a woman. I felt he would refuse to let me help. It was an unspoken and tacit agreement that we would remain together.

One day when we were strolling the markets, he met an old school friend of his. He introduced me as his fiancé. I was shocked as he had not said as much to me. I made no comment at the time, but later asked him why he said that,

"Because, one day I will marry you… you *will* be my wife."
He also said that he should be responsible for me as a good
man should for his wife. He went on to say that he hoped
to make up for all the bad men who had not taken their
responsibility seriously. When he said that, it made me want
to help him even more. I had my savings and there was no
point in them sitting in the bank. I had noticed that there
were also regular deposits into my account from Jinrong.
These far exceeded the funds she owed me for funding the
club. I believed that Jintao was trustworthy, and that brought
me back to the thought where I had stopped trusting people,
'We have to trust people, to live a life of not trusting would
be a sad life,' I thought. So I was prepared to invest in him,
and trust, another person.

One night I decided to tell him what I had been planning.
It was my turn to cook, and he was at the computer, half
writing and half chatting to me. It was winter, with ice
on the streets but we were snug and warm inside, and the
emanating aromas evoked a pleasant atmosphere. As the
food simmered, I went and sat on his lap, and put my arms
around him. He responded and wrapped his arms around
me and kissed me. I leaned back, and took my phone out of
my pocket. I started working the keys.

"What are you doing?" "Hang on", I said, "You'll see in a
sec." I then showed him the face of the screen.

He studied this with confusion, "Whose bank account is
this? Wow, they have a lot of money, 300000RMB."

"It's ours." "Ours? What do you mean... ours?" "This is my bank account, and what is mine is yours. Now that you know it's there, and how much it is, I would like you to think about using it to start a business. After all, you do not like your job, or what you do, and as you're so smart, you would do well in business".

When he started to protest that he could not use my money, I said in jest, "Okay... I'm heading back to the river".

He laughed, "You're serious, aren't you, about the money I mean, not the river?"

"Absolutely, and about as serious as you saying that you want to marry me. My life is yours... you are so good to me. I really don't know how to thank you... Anyway, come to the table, dinner is ready, let's eat and chat about it".

We sat down at the table and I continued, "I want you to think about what sort of business you would like to run, and we will work towards it. I know business, I have run a successful business, and I know financial management... and, another thought, let's find another apartment, one that is bigger and more comfortable for us both... one where we can set up an office space".

He pondered as he ate, until he said, "It would be good to make our own money, and any money we make would go into our own finances... I swear, I will repay you. You say I have been good to you... you are so good to me".

Hearing this, my heart tumbled, and I covered his mouth to interrupt his words. I had tears in my eyes as I said, "Our lives are for each other".

His reply was, "Why are you helping me... why do you always trust?" "Because when I love, I put every part of me into the relationship, nothing is left out".

He stood up from the table, and came and knelt next to me and said, "When are we getting married?" We smiled into each other's eyes. I stood, held out my hand for his, which he took. I led him up to the bed and we made love.

CHAPTER 24
OUR FOUR SEAS

The next morning, still in bed, he murmured, "A restaurant... I want to run a restaurant. As you know, I have loved cooking since childhood. For me to have a restaurant, is a dream I have always had but never thought I would get".

That is what I'd hoped he would say, but it wasn't up to me to influence his decision. I wanted it to come from him. He clearly had an extraordinary sense of food and flavors. He was an exquisite craftsman, which convinced me that he had what it takes to be a successful restaurateur.

I jumped out of bed and grabbed the notebook I had bought for us to start planning our business, where we excitedly started to imagine our new restaurant. As it took shape, we squealed with delight and anticipation, like children planning a holiday camp. We looked at a budget, and my finances. It wasn't quite enough, but then he surprised me when he told me that he too had been saving, on his meager salary, and together, with good bargaining we could just get by. When I started the business with Jinrong, we had taken out that loan with high interest, I didn't want to do that again, I was determined to scrape by without one.

Because of who he was, and his honesty, he insisted that we be full partners and my signature would be required on all business documents. I didn't care. I just wanted to see him happily fulfilled. We decorated and set up the restaurant together, but I allowed him make all the decisions. He did acknowledge my previous experience in many areas and often asked my opinion. He was a dedicated and busy worker, always fully motivated. It warmed my heart to watch him fulfill his dream, and he remained a responsive partner to me and was always most tender.

The restaurant was about 200 square meters, with 80 seats, and was finally completed. The layout was bright and friendly but not ostentatious. Everything was basic, with no frills. The focus was to be on the food. The cuisine was mostly Cantonese, which always leaves a delightful aftertaste. He had created exquisite posters of dishes, which he said would stimulate the appetite of the diners.

The kitchen was located in the corner, opposite the restaurant counter. When patrons entered they could see into the kitchen, which was surrounded by transparent glass, so they were able to watch the chef preparing their food with zest and finesse. The hygiene of the kitchen was of paramount importance to Jintao, and he personally trained all the staff and imbued them with the same professionalism and love for food as he had – and often using the same terms and examples as his uncle had used.

At the start of the process we discussed the name of the restaurant. In the movie *"Kung Fu Kitchen God"*, the restaurant is called Sihai Yipin (Four oceans), so that became the name.

The opening of Sihai Yipin was a joyful occasion. Jintao invited his friends and family, who all proudly came to support him. His uncle, who was now very old, fussed over everything so proudly and with a big grin permanently on his face. Unfortunately Jintao's parents could not make it as they had a school function. The food was like a banquet.

Jintao had spent quite a lot of money on promoting the restaurant, which I had thought was extravagant, given our tight budget, but I was wrong. He said, "If a wine merchant doesn't break open a wine jar, how do people know how good the wine is?" All his promotional activity paid off and he quickly established a credible reputation.

The patrons came, although not many in the initial stages, but each week with the promotional material and word of mouth, their numbers grew. Soon, if people wanted a table on a specific date, they would have to book three days in advance.

When he was in the restaurant, especially in the kitchen, he was like a well versed actor on a stage, knowing all the lines, or like a juggler who is fluid with making the right moves. After having run a successful business before, I was still able to learn things from him.

It was Jintao who went to the markets to buy the ingredients. He would not delegate this to anyone else, not even his head chef. He inspected the produce as if they were the finest silks, to ensure freshness and flavor. I was proud of what I had released within him. It was always there, and would have burst out at some stage, but I was glad that it was I who undid the unwrapping. To see a person I love, fulfilled was a blessing.

CHAPTER 25
TIME OF MILK AND HONEY

We worked hard for more than three months, and the business continued to prosper. It did not take long for the original investment to be recouped. From this we bought our own apartment to eliminate rent, and as an investment. With the passing of time his staff got more and more competent. Again, Jintao had another philosophy, one based on his interest in people – where he gave them more responsibility when he saw potential in them. He felt that when employees have a say in the way things are done, then they will rise to the occasion, and this is what happened. This gave him the chance to relax a bit, after the original stressful pace that he had worked. This was lovely, as we were able to spend quality time together, where our feelings for each other deepened more and more.

We set a date for our marriage, and were working on plans for the wedding. Of course, the main celebration would be in the restaurant, where it would be closed to the general public on the day, but what a celebration it was going to be. I wanted this to happen with all my being, especially when he said that he did not want to wait to have a child.

As much as I believed in our future, I still had ever present fears that something bad was going to happen because of the way every happy event in my life had been sabotaged. One day he noticed these concerns in my heart. He slowly took my hands in his and kissed them gently, and reassured me that it would all work out well. We would be married and we would have two beautiful children – a boy and a girl.

I was also worried that my ugly past would get out and I would become an embarrassment to him. Again, he reassured me that he didn't care who knew about the secrets in my past and it would not change anything between us. When he had finished speaking, he pulled a funny face for me. I was laughing and crying at the same time, I was touched by his adoration. My eyes were wet with happy tears. This is probably the only time in my life that I was speechless. At last, Life had given me a good man who loves me, no matter what.

We took a few weeks off to go and respect our families by telling them of our intention to wed. We tossed a coin as to which set of parents we would see first. I lost the toss, and we would see mine first. I was ashamed that I have not seen my parents for such a long time. I was embarrassed for the disgraceful things I did to disrespect them. Now, I had to stand face to face with them, not knowing what to expect.

No matter how angry we were with each other, they had given me life. It was my responsibility to bow my head to them. I wondered if they were still in the old home, and more so, if they were okay? I had sent them a short letter, ahead of the visit, but had not had time enough to receive a reply. As always *my man* supported me and assured me that everything would work out for the best.

We took the flight from Guangdong to Shandong, spanning more than half of China. From the airport we hired a car and drove to Dongying. The village had not changed, perhaps one or two new buildings had been added. I asked Jintao to drive slowly as I remembered times of my childhood. I was introspective and he respected that with his own silence. Many of the mud brick houses were empty, as the people had gone to the cities to find work. After ten minutes we arrived at their house. I said I wanted to sit for a moment as I was scared of what I had to face. He took my hand as I stared at the old house, flooded with memories. I was not to have silence for long as my parents had been anxiously waiting for us, and came running out the front door. I have never seen my mother with such a big smile. Suddenly, my Mother was standing in front of me. With tears of joy she grabbed and held me tight. She could not stop saying, "My Daughter... Murong... Murong... You are home, you are home!"

Then my father's face was in front of me... his eyes looking into my eyes. His normal reserved demeanor had given way to absolute joy. All three of us now embraced with tears of elation glistening our cheeks. I pulled Jintao into the circle, and the four of us held each other tightly, as I introduced Jintao into the family. My parents insisted on carrying our luggage into the house... they had aged, and I felt riddled with guilt.

When inside, Mother immediately started the tea ceremony, and gave us freshly brewed green tea. There was no real conversation, just excited exclamations, non stop. Every time I looked at Mother, I caught her looking back at me. There was a wanderlust in her eyes that only a mother of one child can show. It was love, pride, and deep joy. As for my father, he was showing Jintao around, and unfortunately also showing him the family photos. I had promised him that would not happen, and I whispered, "Sorry". He just chuckled. He was happy to be seeing the young me, as I was when I was pure and innocent.

Certainly my return was grander than when I left. I handed out many gifts for my parents and relatives. Sadly, I learned that I would never see my grandmother or grandfather again as both of them had passed on. I felt a deep tinge of regret and quivered with sadness.

Looking into the family area, I saw that an extensive feast had been prepared for my homecoming. My heart opened with gladness as I knew that many of my favorites would be waiting for me on that table. I was so proud to have Jintao with me and happy that he was there to finally meet my family.

There was a knock on the door, and a small crowd burst in — it was as if there was a festival, and indeed there was. I knew all of these people. I was a child, and they were now old. I was not expecting all this attention. They surged in, like a wave upon a beach, where each one came and greeted me, touching me and patting me on the back. One old lady, who I remembered as an auntie of the village, took my face in her hands and studied the lines on my face, then looked into my eyes to see who I had become, as if the face tells all.

Where there was once a rebellious teenager, there was now a woman. She must have been satisfied, as she smiled and gave my chin a pat with her hand.

As much as I wanted to eat the beautiful foods, I was too wound up, too excited, and so even with a house full of people wishing to spend time with me, I asked my father, "Father, will you come and walk with me... Let's go to the forest".

We sat on a log, and were quiet, until I started to say, "Father, I am so sorr..." He put a finger against my lips, and said, "Murong, you were and still are the apple of our eye, and you do not have to say anything about those times... In fact, we wished we had seen you sooner so we could apologize for our harsh attitude towards you... We should have been more supportive". We both had tears in our eyes and I had a huge lump in my throat as we walked back, arm in arm.

Back at the house, when all the villagers had gone, father took Jintao outside to chat. They seemed to get on well. I helped Mother clean up and we spoke about my wedding. She said by marrying Jintao I would be honoring the family. She was filled with joy. I told her that the honor would be extended some time into the future with a grandchild for them.

We stayed there for a week, and Jintao was greatly respected by my parents. He, in turn, would respect and honor them as his new parents. By calling them Mother and Father, my Mother was relieved when she saw how well he treated me.

When we went to Jintao's parents, sadly, the uncle had gone to his ancestors. Although his parents showed a liking for me, I was worried because they did not know my past – if they did, I didn't think they would be supportive for their son to marry me? They knew I was five years older than him, which already went against Chinese customs. Jintao was like a bright pearl in their eyes, and as their only child, they would not have wanted their son to be with a woman like me.

After a frantic month, of exhausting wedding preparations, we were married. As a married man, he was even more loving than when he was my boyfriend. It was unheard of... I had the best husband in the whole of China.

CHAPTER 26
SEPARATION IN HAPPINESS

I was a married woman. After so many years of sorrow, I had finally found someone who deserved my total love and devotion. In the eyes of the greater Chinese public, we could walk with respect. This moment was the most fulfilled I had felt in my life.

Our honeymoon was spent in a luxury cabin on a cruise ship as we toured the mighty Yangtze River. The wide, brown, snaking river and delta was like a mirror of my soul... flowing in peace as I relaxed on the slurping waters.

When we returned home, we moved straight into our new apartment and settled in comfortably, as husband and wife. He suggested that I go off the pill immediately and wanted to start trying to conceive our first child. Where before I had castigated Life, I now thanked it for all the lessons in my past and for the joy I had now discovered. A year passed and still there was no child but there was much happiness and we remained enamored with each other. I was concerned that both the abortion and the abuse I suffered at the hands of that brute in the villa, had irreparably damaged my insides.

Jintao expanded the restaurant business and wanted to explore supplying *difficult to find* ingredients to other outlets.

This would entail him travelling to out of the way parts of the country to source new products. I was against it and felt it was unnecessary as we were already doing so well.

When he first suggested this, my eye started twitching... an old familiar warning, but as the months went by, I put it behind me. He was only away for a day or two a month. He then decided he wanted to buy a farm and grow our own produce, organically.

I reasoned, "We have enough of everything we could wish for, and we are blessed. Why are you looking for more?" He shrugged his shoulders and continued working on his computer... writing, I thought. He seemed driven, and I felt there was something in the back of his mind, he wasn't sharing with me. Yet, he was just as loving and respectful as always. My eyes began twitching often at this stage and I felt a growing unease.

As time went by, he became was more and more preoccupied with what I thought, was his writing. I never read it, unless he invited me to. Now I was tempted to spy on him for a clue as to what was going on in his mind but I could not commit that deceit. I convinced myself, I must be grateful that we had each other and were happy.

At that time, there were riots in East Turkistan in the Xinjiang Province, with ongoing looting and burning of property. The workers had been incited to rebel against the local government. Although this was a concern as people were dying or being injured, we were many hundreds of miles away, and with the business, I did not pay much attention to it but I could see that Jintao was disturbed for the people involved. He would watch the news bulletins often, and watch updates on the Internet.

One day he sprang a new business trip on me. He told me he was going to Yunnan to source some new ingredients, "I'll be away about six days".

"Six days! Do you have to go that long?" "It will pass quickly," he reassured me, "...and when I return it will be with some of that lovely Norton Ham that you love so much".

'Why?' I asked myself. I couldn't help thinking of my past partners and their betrayals. I was worried because of the persistent eye twitching, but I never interfered in the business, and no matter what, I was not going to start now.

When he said goodbye to leave for the trip, he seemed reluctant, and held me especially tight, and for a long time. He said, "Six days should be enough", then hesitating, "... but if I don't return after eight days, I have a gift for you. It is in the box at the bedside, but promise me, you won't open it until then".

"What is it?" I asked a confused.

"Just a little present for my wife... and sorry Murong, on this farm where I'm going there is not likely to be an Internet connection so I may not be able to call or message you". Then he was gone.

I was steeped in misery. My eyes were twitching and I felt helpless. My man was doing something suspicious that he would not talk about. All I could do was trust him and wait. I was lost and lonely as we had now been together for nearly three years and had only spent a few nights apart. Thinking about him, looking out at the bright moon, hanging in the sky, outside the window, I prayed that he would come back within the six days and that I would feel silly for doubting him.

I did try to call him, but there was never an answer. I kept calling him, and it was frustrating and I was beside myself with worry.

After the third night, I could not sleep and nightmares troubled me. I dreamed that Jintao never returned to me. When I woke up, I tried to tell myself that these were just foolish dreams. Every time I fell asleep the dreams returned. At 3.00 am I bolted upright, in a cold sweat. Something terrible had happened. I could feel it. I got up and paced the bedroom floor. I was in an absolute panic. I phoned his parents and asked them if they had heard anything. They did not even know he had gone away, and were concerned. I tried to go back to sleep but the pillow was soaked with sweat and tears.

I turned on the TV as a distraction and soon a news bulletin came on. There was more trouble in East Turkistan. The news reader spoke about an unnamed hero of the country. He was some sort of undercover agent in the East Turkistan riots, and it was he who had provided the authorities with inside information on the ringleaders. From this, the Xinjiang police successfully arrested thirty-two terrorists. However, when the hero had been identified by the terrorists, he was killed. They said his service to his country was a glorious sacrifice. 'Jintao will be saddened by this as he loves China', I thought to myself.

There was one thing that kept coming to the forefront of my mind, and it gave me great comfort... our lovemaking the evening before he left. Our love making was always lovely, but this time seemed more special and deeper for some reason. He held on to me tightly with strong emotion, yet with so much tenderness. His ejaculation within me seemed stronger, more intense, washing over me with our powerful love. Our emotions were so strong that they brought a combination of tears and laughter. We fell asleep with him still inside me, and our arms wrapped around each other. In a strange way, I felt that this was the only thing I had to hang on to.

I tried to comfort myself, and convince myself that Jintao would return safely and that I would feel silly for putting myself through so much turmoil, but I could not quieten the disease inside of me. I could not shake off the dreams and the continual twitching of my eyes and the disturbance I felt when I woke up at 3.00 am traumatized and sweating.

It seemed like an eternity before the eighth day arrived. In my worry, I had forgotten about the present beside the bed, but now it all came back to me. I needed something to hold on to, so ran to the box and tore off the wrapping. Inside there was a letter and an MP3.

There was only one song on the MP3, '*So close, so far* (by Jacky Cheung). This is one of Jintao's favorite songs. I listened as I opened the letter, with shaking hands.

To My beautiful Murong:

If you are reading this letter, I may not be in this world anymore. I know that you will be angry, perhaps hating me, as the deeper love is, the more reason to be angry. I am sorry as there are many promises that I made, which I now cannot fulfill, such as protecting you, and being another man who has left you with pain in your belly. But the biggest broken promise was to not make our child.

I have gone to the trouble in East Turkistan... (As I read this, I remembered the news bulletin, and my heart missed a beat... no, not the dead hero!) *You are probably wondering that if I love you so much, why did I do this to jeopardize our love, to be yet another one that hurts you. I can only answer – do you remember the night when I took you to my house? Over time, you told me about your past, and you did this without reservation. Even if you dismissed those things, the more I listened, the angrier I got. I hid it but my emotions were out of control. I really wanted to hurt those people who hurt you. I respected your strength of character, where even at the potential loss of our relationship you told me the truth. Now that I have you as my wife, and hopefully one day children, I feel that I must protect you, and all our Chinese family. It is my duty to do so. I have to do what I feel I must do. I cannot hide from who I am – you taught me that.*

My love, you were the best gift life has given me. In my eyes, you are the most authentic person in the world. My love for you is all encompassing.

Our love is so important, but this, what I am about to do is even more so. I hope you understand.

According to Taoist philosophy; martyrs who are inspired to do things for the people, become immortalized. You know me better than that, I don't care about being immortalized, but I do what I have to do for now, and our people. Either way, after death, if that happens, I will be happy in heaven or wherever I end up. And hopefully, one day when you are old you will join me – I will wait.

With all the love of the universe within me, I shower it on you. I will not say goodbye, as it is not a "final goodbye", but be happy my love, until we join in love and devotion once again…
Jintao.

I was sobbing while listening to the music and reading. I wanted to scream with anger. I did not want to understand any of this…. My heart was crushed like a clay pot. How, for one minute, could he have imagined that this suicide note would be a present for me? Men… Aaarrrrrrrgh! It felt like a sick joke… a torture too difficult to bear.

I realized why he had spent so much time, obsessed on the Internet. He was not   researching his book but was following those horrific events. He must have been in direct contact with the secret service and offered his services to help quell the violence.

A knock at the door disturbed my thoughts. It was the police. They came in and asked me to sit down and broke the news to me that Jintao was dead. They told me he was a hero of the people and would be decorated and buried with full honors. The time of his death seemed to correspond to the time I woke up in the middle of the night in a frantic panic.

I collapsed on to the settee, gasping for air and sobbing. They waited, patiently for me to compose myself, then they asked me to go with them to Xinjiang to identify the body of Lai Jintao. They had a plane waiting and I needed to leave in a hurry. Dazed, I threw a few things into a bag, grabbed my jacket off the coat stand and followed them out. At times my knees gave way and they had to support me. My heart felt like it had been stabbed by a knife that was being twisted, deeper and deeper. I was shaking uncontrollably, thinking, 'No... no...no this can't be real...this can't be true!'

When I saw Jintao lying peacefully in the transparent coffin, with his eyes closed and hands folded over his chest, I broke down. My legs were like rubber, and again they had to hold me upright. They held me as I touched his cold, youthful face, screaming, I shudder upon touching his cold body. "Jintao, why did you do this? You betrayed our love? You promised me you would always be there for me and never leave me, like the others did. You promised from that day on I would have happiness in my life. How can I live alone in this world without you? Why? You lied... I hate you! I want to die with you... to join you in death".

They had to forcefully coax me away, and took me to a hotel for the night. A doctor prescribed a strong sedative, so I slept, but I was in and out of a delirium. When I awoke, my eyes were swollen and painful. I was numb with grief. I didn't think about food all day, but they encouraged me to eat. Again, Life had chosen to destroy my life. The last time it did this, it was Jintao who saved me, but now he has been taken him from me. He is gone, and I had to live without him. There seemed to be no point to these snippets of happiness that always ended in destruction. Life without him would be like a black hole… shallow and empty.

His parents who had arrived, encouraged, "Murong, we hope that you will still be able to find happiness in this life. He would have wanted you to live". His mother held me, trying to feed life into me. She continued encouraging me, "Although he has gone… his short life was filled with success and hope. He was happy with his achievements, and would have no regrets. He loved you… you made him happy. His love for you turned into a greater love for the good of his country. He died, so others could live. By doing so, Jintao proudly took on this mission, that only he could understand.' She began lighting joss sticks and held them to her heart. She handed me one as she continued with the sacred ritual. She placed another joss stick into the bed of the urn, "We should glorify him in death and be proud of him", she said as the smoke filled the air, the scent my nostrils. All I could think of was, 'Jintao, you were a foolish and idealistic man'.

Jintao's body was buried in his hometown, Maoming. I stood stoically beside his tomb, and was reluctant to leave. Later, back at his parent's home, where I was to stay for a few days, I was broken… a walking corpse… empty with nothing left inside me. Most of the time I hid away in my room, the same room that Jintao had grown up in. It was bursting with him as a child – school projects, books, models of planes and war ships. As I stared at photos of him, in his school uniform, my heart was soaked in sorrow, for my loss and for the children we would never have.

CHAPTER 27
GRIEF FLOODS

It seemed that I had cried for an eternity and been in pain for my entire life, and that there could be no more tears to cry or agony to break me – still, they were unstoppable... a steady stream of both. How could I carry on like this... myself a ghost... there was no purpose left. I remember the words of Kahlil Gibran, '*And ever has it been that love knows not its own depth until the hour of separation*'. There was no reason for life, and if Jintao was right, then the sooner I go to meet him in death, the better it would be for both of us... why keep him waiting? ... And that is where you found me Enzo, on that bridge, ready to tumble into death so I could join my husband. I told you that you could never understand my pain and suffering. Now you have the whole of what I have endured, and what I do not want to endure again... There is no point in living, and so very soon I shall return to the bridge... you can't stop me, or keep me locked up, and if you are half human, you will release me to do what I must do".

Enzo had quietly listened to her painful account of the horrors of her life, over those past few days. Many times he had tears in his eyes. Many times she saw him hiding his face in his hands, in disbelief of how much one woman can suffer in the search for love. He rose up off the chair and put a supportive hand on her shoulder, and for a full two minutes said nothing. He just stood there, then he spoke gently, "No, Murong, I will not stop you going back to the river. It is your right to do this if this is what you want, and it is not my right to take control your of your destiny. All I ask is that you delay it. Stay here with myself and my family for a few weeks. Allow us to love and heal you. Then, if one day you quietly disappear we will understand. For now, grieve in this house and compose yourself before you make your mind up to join your husband. Please will you do this for us… for yourself?"

It was then she noticed his wife, Feiru, and his daughter Sangru were in the room. They both came over to her and put their arms around her. Murong buckled over and wept.

Sangru said, "I love you my sister, I am here for you".

Feiru added, "And you will be my second daughter… this house will always be open to you".

The woman embraced her, in silence, as they rubbed her back and arms with affection, allowing her pain to emerge as it needed. After a while, she nodded in confirmation that she would not do anything drastic for a few weeks, while she tried to find a place inside of her that wanted to heal. They cocooned her tighter in their love.

CHAPTER 28
THE SUN SHINES

For three days she lay in her room, only coming out to go to the bathroom. They brought her meals in, and took turns to sit with her, holding her, but saying little. At times they gave her space to be alone with her pain, but were always close by to watch over her. On the fourth day she came out and spent some time with them.

The pain lessened a little bit each day, and she forced the future away from her mind, as she decided to live each day as it came. Over the days, while she was recovering, her mind was like a movie playing, over and over, all the things that Jintao and she shared together... his initial shyness, at how young he was, and how he was stunned when she asked him for shelter. She thought of the restaurant, which was still running under the good care of his staff, and about his letter and ultimate sacrifice, and what a good man he was. She particularly remembered their last night of love making.

Enzo said in one of their chats, "Jintao was a man among men. You should be proud of what he did".

Two weeks later she woke up one morning with the trace of a smile on her face. Her period was three weeks late, and she had an image, in her mind of a young plant, with tiny shoots, strongly striving to reach up through the earth, to the light. With determination she suppressed the hope of what this could mean... could it be... if only it would be... She went to Feiru and asked her if she could buy her a pregnancy test kit. With a grin from ear to ear, Feriu immediately rushed to the chemist and bought one. Thirty minutes later their smiles were bigger. "Quick", Feiru said, "get ready, we are going to my doctor for confirmation".

As she dressed she heard Feriu phone her doctor, and heard her browbeating the receptionist to make an appointment for her immediately. Twenty minutes later they were in her doctor's rooms. As the test was being done, Murong and Feiru held hands, Feiru's eyes smiling into Murong's. The doctor finally said, "Mrs. Lai, you are six weeks pregnant, congratulations".

That night was a celebration. Joy descended on all. Enzo and his family cooked Murong a special meal, and they drank Champaign. She phoned her parents, and Jintao's, to share the wonderful news. Enzo and his family demanded that she stay with them until the birth.

Seven and a half months later a chubby, healthy baby girl cried her way into the world. Murong gave her the name of Yuqing Jintao Lai. She could immediately see that she had Jintao's eyes and his clear skin color, and of course, his blood and his genes were coursing through her little body. Murong hoped that she would inherent his uncomplicated way.

She made Enzo, Yuqing's Godfather, and Feiru, Godmother, and invented a new title for Sangu as God-Auntie. So with grand, and God parents, this child would never be short of loving relatives. Murong was determined to bring the child up surrounded in love, and let her know that her father was a great hero before his death...

Later, mother and child, moved back home, to the apartment. She spent some time at the restaurant, but mainly left it to run by the staff. When she and little Yuqing were there, there was always staff around to hold and coo over the baby. Murong set up a staff profit sharing, where a portion of the profit went into a fund for the staff. The admin and accounts were given to a new bookkeeper, but Murong did an audit every so often... just to keep her on her toes.

In order to memorialize Jintao, and to pay tribute to such a hero, she set up a foundation, and each month a part of the restaurant's profit was donated to the foundation to help those people who had been maimed or made husbandless in that tragedy. It was called The Lai Jintao foundation. "My husband will be remembered for the person he was", She insisted.

At the opening, in a loud and clear voice she said, "Life gave me the best and most loving husband a wife could wish for, and in God's compassion he gave us a daughter. What reason can I now have to be sad or to cry?"

She made contact, with all the people who had molded her life, starting in the order of meeting them, Hong Ge, then Liu Jen, and Jinrong. She took baby Yuqing and thanked them for the part that they had played in her life. She wished them nothing but harmony in their own lives.

Murong took Yuqing to Mount Lotus, and carried her in a backpack. Together wife and daughter of Jintao, climbed the mountain. At the top, she spoke to Yuqing about her namesake, Yuqing, and introduced them to each other. It was a cloudy day, but as she did this, the clouds parted and the sun shone through, with a wide searching beam.

The end

www.ingramcontent.com/pod-product-compliance
Lightning Source LLC
Chambersburg PA
CBHW030429120726
47903CB00003B/882